# CAPTAIN SUPERLATIVE

# Captain Superlative

by J. S. Puller

Disney • HYPERION
Los Angeles New York

First Hardcover Edition, May 2018
First Paperback Edition, February 2019
3 5 7 9 10 8 6 4 2
FAC-025438-19172
Printed in the United States of America

This book is set in 12-pt Sabon LT Pro, ITC Franklin Gothic,
Rockwell Std/Monotype; Wanderlust Letters/Fontspring
Designed by Phil Caminiti and Maria Elias

Library of Congress Cataloging-in-Publication Control
Number for Hardcover Edition: 2017033488
ISBN 978-1-368-00563-0

Visit www.DisneyBooks.com

The SFI label applies to the text stock

For my favorite superheroes, my parents—
Deborah Goldberg and Neil Puller

# Captain Superlative

# Prologue

**We released paper lanterns into the** night. They floated toward the moon. I don't know who brought them. None of this was planned. We all just found ourselves in the parking lot of Deerwood Park Middle School, sitting on the hoods of SUVs, our legs sticking to the paint in the heat of an Illinois summer. We watched the lanterns dance and twirl, going higher and higher. They were like a school of sky fish, moving together as one.

Captain Superlative would have loved seeing them. And seeing us too. The entire seventh-grade class. Technically eighth graders, and the top of the food chain now that it was July.

Even though she was gone, I heard her voice again.

"I'm going to be a superhero."

I smiled a little bit, imagining that I could feel her warmth and her presence at my side, just behind my shoulder, where she liked to stand. The glittering lanterns turned into the glow-in-the-dark stars stuck to the ceiling of her bedroom. I was almost there with her, like a breeze in the air, watching as she sat on the foot of her bed in pink pj's, her lopsided blue wig on her head like a crown.

"I'm going to be a superhero."

It was her voice, that stubborn and determined voice that sounded so confident that you couldn't help but believe anything she said. She wasn't saying it to anyone, though. Just to herself. She was alone, staring at the wallpaper of cabbage roses.

"I'm going to be a superhero."

That's how I like to believe it began.

Of course, no one knows for sure how it *really* happened. There were plenty of different versions that popped up over the course of the second semester. They were just stories, though. Half-truths and imaginings. Jokes and guesses. They passed from one person to the next, with each listener adding their own special twist to it. Soon the characters—once simple classmates—were bigger than before. Stronger. Better. Superlative.

I think, in her case, maybe the word was justified. She earned the right to be called *superlative.*

"Janey..."

A real voice. A voice in the present tense. Paige's voice. I turned to look at her along the line of my shoulder. The light of the lanterns played against the dark planes of her face and across the tops of her cornrows. She looked angelic, like a little fairy. It was remarkable how much she'd changed since January. She was an entirely different person now, head held high. But I could see the swollen bags under her eyes, the glistening beneath her nose. She was hurting.

We all were.

I slid down from the hood of my dad's car and walked over to Paige. Our arms wrapped around each other's waist and we turned to watch the lanterns together.

"I was thinking about *her* this morning," Paige said, after a few moments of companionable silence.

No need to ask who she was talking about. There was only one *her*.

"Me too," I said. "What about her?"

"Just how it's going to be weird," she said.

"What?"

"Not seeing her here every day."

"Yeah. But she wouldn't want us getting all weepy about it."

Paige let out a small, breathy laugh. "Probably not."

"You know exactly what she would say."

"Something about not wasting time being sad when there was work to be done and citizens in need."

I smiled. "Exactly."

Doors to open and giants to slay. Captain Superlative was so annoyingly set in her ways.

Not everyone can just decide who it is they're going to be. Especially not at the age of twelve. A lot of us need to figure it out over time. And we usually screw it up. More than once.

More than five times. Or ten. The road to figuring out who you are is paved with failures. But that's life.

I guess you could say I speak from some experience. One particular experience, really; a wild ride that began back in January.

# 1

*Ostracism.*

Ms. Hinton scrawled the word across the dry-erase board in thick, faded black strokes, the marker squeaking a little with age. I leaned my chin into my palm, watching the motes of dust dance in a shaft of light from the window overlooking the parking lot. "Does anyone know what this means?"

I knew. It came up the other day when I was watching TV with my dad and he'd explained it to me.

Oddball.

Outlander.

Outsider.

Outcast.

Still, I didn't raise my hand. I just sat at my desk in the back of the room, staring at the dust, trying to keep my expression blank. Counting the motes helped keep me from looking interested. They were sluggish and languid, like the January sunlight was slowly freezing them. Any second and they would come to a complete standstill, fossilized in a single moment of time. The margins of my notebook were carefully filled with idle doodles—wavy lines and patterned polka dots and little stars. I didn't even bother to look at them as I drew, randomly connecting them, creating an abstract shape that meant nothing at all.

It was dangerous to show too much of an interest in class. You'd be labeled as a nerd. I had daydreaming down to a science. I knew exactly how to zone out; just the right amount to fit in with everyone else, while still picking up enough of what the teacher was saying to avoid being grounded by my dad for getting a C or a D. The middle of the pack was the safest place, never rushing too far forward.

Paige McCoy was the only one to raise her hand, fingers twitching slightly in the air.

"Yes, Paige?" Ms. Hinton said.

"Ostracism is when you get kicked out," Paige said. She had a thin voice, one that always sounded tired.

"Yes." Ms. Hinton nodded curtly. "The idea was invented by the ancient Greeks, the Athenians to be specific. Who, as I hope you remember from before winter break, came up with a crazy little thing we like to call 'democracy.' Ostracism was a big part of their democracy. It was temporary banishment by popular vote. Usually of citizens that others considered dangerous to the state. Can you imagine that? Everyone coming together to vote someone out of the city?"

Dagmar Hagen's manicured hand shot up. "Ms. Hinton?"

"Yes?"

"Was there any way to argue against the vote?" she asked. "Or if you were voted out, did that mean you couldn't come back?"

"Citizens were allowed to come back after ten years," Ms. Hinton said, delighted that Dagmar had asked the question. Dagmar was every teacher's favorite—daughter of the woman who'd led Deerwood Park's champion cheerleading squad twenty years ago and a perfect straight-A student. Dagmar had followed in her mother's competitive footsteps and led the sixth-grade soccer team to victory last summer—giving us incredible bragging rights over our rivals at Kohn Junior High—and was destined to do the same this year. It seemed like Ms. Hinton always had a special smile reserved just for Dagmar. "But that didn't mean they couldn't be voted out again."

"So could the people just keep kicking someone out again and again until they got the message?"

"Yes. Absolutely."

"That is so *sad*!"

Ms. Hinton laughed and turned to write the definition on the board.

Dagmar's eyes cut over to Paige. It was clear who Dagmar had in mind to vote out of the city, but I doubted Paige cared at this point. It was just a way of life.

The bell rang.

Everyone dragged themselves to their feet, shoving social-studies books haphazardly into bags. The sound of plastic Blue Shoes squeaked on the tiles. Ms. Hinton knew better than to try to get another word in. She shook her head and waved us out the door, calling, "Dagmar, say hello to your mother for me. Tell her I hope she had a good holiday."

"I will!"

And then Ms. Hinton sat behind her desk and started flipping through her planner, going into the secret realm of meditation that all teachers seemed to know about.

The second her back was turned, Dagmar ripped a sheet out of her notebook with slow, careful exactness. We could hear the holes in the paper tear away from each ring of the binder. She leaned over, writing Paige's name across the blue lines in her neat, extra-curly handwriting. Casually, she crumpled it up, tossing it behind her with expert precision. The paper bounced off Paige's shoulder as Dagmar glided out of the classroom, her minions flocking after her like moths to a flame.

What a pair they were, Dagmar and Paige. Complete opposites. Where Dagmar was light, Paige was dark. Where Dagmar was tall, Paige was short. Where Dagmar was fire, Paige was earth.

Paige didn't even look at the sheet of paper. She let it slough off into a corner as she collected her books, balanced them precariously in her arms, and ducked out into the hallway.

She wouldn't be any safer out there, I thought, looping the strap of my bag over my shoulder. Not when Dagmar had followers around her. And Dagmar always had followers, for one reason or another. Sometimes, they gathered to laugh through a hashtag on her phone, which should have been kept in her locker, as per the rules of the school. Sometimes it was under the irrational hope that some of her "cool" would rub off. Or else, it was to avail themselves of her "charitable" giving. She'd just won the school service award for student tutoring. Teachers thought she was some kind of angel on a quest to help those less fortunate or less attentive in class, but most of us knew the truth. Dagmar only helped the girls on the soccer team with their homework. You couldn't be on the team with bad grades. Dagmar's "selflessness" meant that they all passed their classes, so they could all stay together and so that no one else could join.

Dagmar was single-handedly holding the championship team together, and they knew it. The moths worshiped the ground she fluttered above. Really, everyone who wanted to stick it to Kohn Junior High did too.

Which was pretty much everyone.

I could already hear the peals of laughter from Dagmar and her friends. The moths had all copied Dagmar, writing Paige's name on sheets of paper and throwing them at Paige as she passed by with her head down. It was a pity we weren't the ancient Greeks. At least then, Paige could have escaped to the blissful isolation of exile. But here? Paige was being voted out of the city with nowhere to go. And no doubt, as Dagmar suggested, she would be voted out again and again.

I waited until everyone cleared the room before I trudged through the doorway, so that they wouldn't see me. Then again, no one ever really saw me. I was as unimportant as air. And equally invisible.

Intangible.

Insignificant.

*Inconsequential*, a wonderful new word I'd recently picked up from my dad.

It was better that way.

It was just after winter break. The freshly cleaned halls echoed with the sound of friends filling in friends about their holiday adventures. The halls were also dotted with lost, confused faces. January always brought about a wave of new kids. They popped up like dandelions, usually the kids of military families from the active fort on the edge of Deerwood Park.

It was easy to pick them out. They had maps—and they hadn't gotten their Blue Shoes yet.

Drifting through the halls that morning, I noticed something else. Something I'd never felt before—a buzz mixed with the usual slamming of lockers, the usual shuffling of feet, the usual begging Dagmar to sneak a peek at the latest cat video. All of that tended to fade away into a murky cloud of white noise. But not today. There was a thrum in the air, like a vibrating guitar string. Kids were talking. They were talking about something exciting. Something that managed to break into my solitude.

At first, I thought it might be the anticipation of the Valentine's Day dances. They were over a month away, but already there were pink and red and purple flyers littering the walls, covered in goopy hearts and little fat cupids, aiming arrows at one another. The rules had changed this year. The sixth- and seventh-grade dances were going all the way to ten o'clock. And the eighth-grade dance would last until eleven. Any change like that would have called for gossip and excitement.

But it wasn't about the dances.

"You will not believe what I just saw."

I recognized the voice. Tyler Jeffries. He was standing with a group of seventh-grade boys, just outside the gym locker rooms.

Tyler Jeffries pretty much *was* Deerwood Park Middle School. Smart, funny, gorgeous, and talented. He was the highlight of every school play. He stole every scene. Kids hung on his every word, every note. I couldn't wait to see him in the spring production of *Beauty and the Beast*. He was playing Gaston. A part that was all wrong for him, in my opinion. A boy like him was a boy who got the girl in the end. As far as I was concerned, Tyler Jeffries was a Greek god. Better, really. Greek gods had *flaws*. Tyler Jeffries was perfect. Everyone thought so, and I was no exception.

Tyler Jeffries's sandy-brown hair and speckled hazel eyes were the object of most people's attention. But not mine. I was obsessed with the arch of his upper lip. It's strange, I know, but that lip made me think of the perfect bend in a Persian archer's bow. Or the top of a heart. I was forever drawing it in the margins of my notebook. I dreamed of Tyler Jeffries launching a fatal kiss at me.

Nothing else could get my heart racing so much.

Or at all.

When Tyler Jeffries was interested in something, it was worth noting. That was the rule. I strained to hear what it was he was saying to his friends. "What did you see, pretty boy?" one of them asked.

"It was the weirdest thing ever," he said.

"Weirder than your dance moves?"

"Hey now. I'm an *artist*."

"Maybe an abstract artist."

"You're just jealous," Tyler said, throwing his arms up in the air and flailing them like a Muppet. It was more like he was swatting a swarm of flies than dancing, but somehow he made it work.

The boys laughed. "Keep telling yourself that," one said.

They disappeared into the locker room, chuckling and teasing, the battered wooden door swinging shut behind them and their excitement.

*What had he seen?*

The next passing period, the hallway hum returned.

Dagmar and her best friend, April Cormack, were standing side by side in front of the wooden trophy case near the gym, scrolling through something on Dagmar's phone. In their matching soccer-team uniforms and Blue Shoes, they looked like twin backup hip-hop dancers.

Dagmar's curly hair was like a living flame. She always had her head turned to a perfect angle, showing off her best features. It was as if she were expecting everyone in the hall to turn into paparazzi, clamoring to get her picture. Even when she was distracted, she was posing. And something was obviously distracting her. She and April muttered in fury to one another, their heads bunched together.

"You have *got* to be kidding me," Dagmar said.

"Not even a little bit," April said.

"How could anyone even do that?!"

"I know, right?"

That was all I could hear.

It was the same again the next passing period. And the one after that. Soon, even Paige was talking about it. Whatever "it" was.

"Is it really true?" she asked, sidling up beside me.

No one ever asked me anything.

I opened my mouth to reply, to ask what she meant. Too slow. I saw Dagmar and her moths out of the corner of my eye, sweeping down the hall with the speed of a forest fire. Smoothly, I turned, pretending to open the locker to one side. Dagmar blew past me, veering in Paige's direction. "Hey, Paige," she said, eyes demurely looking up from her phone. "This just came up on the news. 'Local Woman Caught Shoplifting from Dollar Store.' There's a picture. Isn't this your mom?"

She turned the screen of her phone in Paige's direction, but Paige stormed past her without looking. "You know that's not my mom," she said.

"Oops," Dagmar replied.

The moths all laughed.

I clutched the charm on my necklace. It was a little silver star with a blue glass bead in the middle that had once belonged to my mother. I wore it every day. As a way to be close to her, I guess. I turned the combination lock on a locker that didn't even belong to me, waiting for everyone to go away.

By the end of the day, I'd almost gotten used to the hum, sinking back into it like the usual, comfortable haze. Whatever the new gossip was, I figured it wouldn't have much influence on my existence. How did you influence the air, anyway?

It was the passing time between eighth and ninth period. The end of the day was in sight. I was at my locker, my *real* locker, when I heard April's shrill voice shriek behind me.

"She's coming this way."

"What?" someone else asked.

"Look, she's down the hall!"

Who was *she*?

I turned around. April was standing five feet away from me, talking to one of Dagmar's other soccer-team flunkies. Meredith, I supposed. Both she and April would have been thrown off the team long ago, but I was pretty sure Dagmar was doing their homework. For a second, they blocked my view, but then they stepped back. Everyone stepped back. The hallway seemed to part down the center, everyone pressing up against the banks of red lockers on either side.

And that was when I caught my first glimpse of *her*.

She wasn't very tall, probably not even five feet. But for some reason, she seemed bigger. She filled the space around her. Her hands were on her hips, her chin up, and her chest forward. It was the same sort of classic stance that I saw on the covers of my dad's comic books. Wide and open. Completely exposed. Unafraid.

Probably a good thing—being unafraid—considering the way she was dressed.

She wore a bathing suit. It was the beginning of a wet and cold January and she looked ready for the beach. The shiny silver suit had thick straps, joined together by silver rings on top of her shoulders. Under it, she had a pair of bright, almost neon-blue tights. There was a hole in the left side, near her ankle, a bit of a rip going up the side of her leg that was only partly hidden by a red high-top sneaker. She also wore blue rubber gloves, the kind my dad used to wash dishes in the kitchen sink. Draped over her shoulders was a red cape, probably made out of a pillowcase, judging from the way it bunched up behind her neck.

Dead silence. I had never heard a school hallway that still. Everyone was staring at her. Everyone.

Time stopped.

I couldn't tell what she was thinking or feeling. A red mask hid her face, the strings of it tied messily behind her head, with strands of the thick neon-blue synthetic hair of a wig caught up in the knot. I could see her mouth, though, her lips curling up into some kind of wicked smile.

"Who are you?" Someone from the crowd asked it. I didn't realize, at first, that it was me.

She turned to me. Everyone did. I wanted to shrink against the locker, maybe even pass through it. The heat of so many eyes was a little more than I could take. The wind had been knocked out of my lungs. Fortunately, the moment she spoke, the attention turned back on her.

"Captain Superlative!" she said, in a voice full of confidence and certainty. "Champion of Deerwood Park Middle School, here to defend honor, justice, and the forces of good!" She made a broad, sweeping gesture with one arm. "Have no fear, citizens!" Both arms went up, fingertips stretched out and pressed together like blades to cut through the air. "Captain Superlative is here to make all troubles disappear!"

She whipped around and shot down the hall, faster than life. Like she was flying. Her cape fluttered in the air behind her, an enormous letter *C* made of blue felt glued on the back.

We stood there in a state of stunned silence, the sort that followed a natural disaster, a tidal wave. Even after she disappeared, we felt her there. It was only the sound of the bell marking the end of the passing period that broke the spell and sent us off in a thousand directions, like motes of dust, whispering about the outfit, the catchphrase, the name, the strangeness of it all.

Speculation spread: It was all for the school play. She'd been hit on the head. She'd been sent by Kohn Junior High. Someone had dared her to do it. It was the start of an alien invasion to replace us with pod people. Each idea was more outlandish than the last. None of it was right. I knew it in my heart of hearts. But I didn't have a theory of my own, beyond what I thought was a reasonable assumption that she had to be a new kid.

What I did have was a sense of wonder.

When no one talks to you, you see everything. What else is there to do but watch the world?

But I didn't understand.

I couldn't understand.

Air understands nothing.

# 2

**Deerwood Park was the town time** forgot. Or at least the town that time didn't visit too often. The biggest excitement we had was a bluebird perching in a raspberry bush. The most color we saw was the rainbows in oil slicks at the gas station. And the only conflict I could recall was the local council debate over a drive-through restaurant. The vote was six to three against—no one needed to get their food that fast.

That was Deerwood Park, and my dad and I lived on the very edge of it, spitting distance from Lake Michigan and the Wisconsin border. When I was younger, we had a big house with a porch swing and flower boxes, a few blocks away from the movie theater and the ice-skating rink. It was straight out of a storybook, or the past, maybe. But we moved into our apartment building when I was nine.

I cried on the day we left. A lot. I remember wrapping my arms around the fifty-year-old maple in the front yard. I begged my dad to let us stay. We *had* to stay. It was too big a change. Too much. Too fast. But my dad put his hand on my shoulder and told me that we had to leave. The house was haunted by a ghost, he said. A ghost that he wanted to leave behind. A ghost we *needed* to leave behind.

Then he'd made me promises. Our new home would be wonderful. We'd make a new start and have a thousand new memories. It would be our very special, secret place. We'd be happy.

He'd been right too (even if I still checked my closet for ghosts for the next year). Our apartment was the still and tranquil center of my little world. It was the one place in the universe where I was happiest.

The one place in the universe where I wasn't air, where I didn't *have* to be.

It was nothing exciting. The carpets were beige and bland, the rooms were average size, but it was enough for us. My dad's bedroom was right next to mine. We used the third bedroom for a study, although there were more board games than books in there. The kitchen was always warm and light, the sunset always filling it with gold around dinnertime. Pictures from the old house that I'd drawn in kindergarten were still on the wheezy yellow refrigerator, their corners curling up with age, like the shoes of a genie in a picture book. We had a table, but my dad and I usually ate dinner on stools, on the far end of the marble island with the stove top. The table just felt so empty with only two people.

It reminded us of the ghost.

"A superhero, huh?" my dad said that night, when I finished telling the tale of Captain Superlative's bracing arrival in the hall.

"I don't know, Dad," I said. "She just showed up. Wearing a cape."

"A cape?"

"With an enormous letter *C* on it. For 'Captain Superlative'"—I used air quotes—"I guess."

My dad grinned, the corners of his eyes crinkling up. I had brown eyes, but my dad's were a deep, dark blue. The color I imagined the ocean to be. When he smiled like that, they became lost under heavy wrinkles and even heavier eyebrows, wires of brown and gray. "Clearly," he said, touching his finger to his ear. It was a gesture that signaled the beginning of one of our many rituals.

"Certainly," I replied, pleased with my word of choice.

"Completely."

I struggled for a moment to come up with another word, but was saved when I remembered my science homework from a few days back. "Conclusively!"

My dad laughed, clapping his hands together once. "Oh! Good one!"

Breaking the pattern was considered a surrender. I grinned with pride at my victory. I didn't win the game often, given my dad's love for words.

After polishing off the last of his green beans, my dad tapped his fork absently against the side of his plate. "Maybe you should start wearing a big letter *J*, Janey," he said.

"Dad!"

He tapped his ear again. "Joking."

"Jesting," I shot back.

"Joshing."

I wrinkled my nose. "Old word."

"Old man," he replied, gesturing to himself.

I couldn't argue with that or with the spirals of silver sparkling in his curly, otherwise brown hair.

He started to launch into a story from the afternoon. He worked as a veterinarian, and most of his stories—which usually ended with a dog peeing on him—had me howling with laughter.

Tonight was different. With a bit of a scowl, I propped my elbow up on the counter, dropping my chin into my palm. I was only half listening, really. His voice sounded like a video whose audio had been sped up so it came out like a squeaking chipmunk. It was one of those nights where even the familiar things couldn't quite get my mind to relax. All throughout my afternoon, as I plodded through my homework and several reruns of this old sitcom my dad loved and had gotten me addicted to, I kept flashing back to the hallway, to Captain Superlative's grand entrance. And I was there again now, watching her swim upstream against the tide in her mask and cape. In my memory, she was the only thing moving. The rest of us were frozen. She was on fast-forward. "I would never do something like that." I don't know why I said it. It wasn't about me. But the words just sort of popped out of my mouth.

"Something like what, Janey?" Dad asked.

"Run around like some kind of superhero."

My dad raised one of his eyebrows. "And why not?"

Well, that was easy enough. "I'd be labeled as a freak in two seconds."

"Ah! The perils of labeling. I remember it well. Some things never change." He stood up, taking my plate and heading for the sink. "And what social circle are you in these days, Jane Esther Silverman?"

I wrinkled my nose. I hated it when he used my full name. It sounded like a little old lady's name. "I don't know."

"You know," he said, glancing over his shoulder at me, "that's why you're my favorite daughter. You're a work in progress."

"And I'm your only daughter."

"Well, that too."

"Unless you count Selina."

"I never count Selina."

Right on cue, with a soft mew, our cat, Selina, padded her way into the kitchen, winding her sinewy, sleek black body around my dad's ankles.

"What about my best friend April?" he asked. "What's her social circle?"

That was an old joke. One that still made me groan. April and I hadn't spoken in years, but back when she was my best friend, my dad always joked that she was really *his* best friend and that she only came over to our house to hear his awful jokes, just pretending that it was to visit me.

"Definitely the popular, pretty, athletic, not-freak circle," I said, standing up and joining him at the sink. He washed the dishes in his thick kitchen gloves while I wiped down the counter with a rag that had once been a T-shirt. He got out the chocolate-chip cookie-dough ice cream while I got out the whipped-cream canister. Just like every night. I thought the subject of Captain Superlative was put to rest.

My dad thought otherwise.

"What do you think her origin story could be?" he asked me as he topped off my two scoops with a noisy squirt of whipped cream.

"What?"

"Your Captain Superlative." He made a vague gesture toward me. As if I owned her. "All good superheroes need an origin story."

"You think?"

"I don't *think*, young lady." He pointed the tip of the whipped-cream canister at me. "I *know*. Don't you remember what my social circle was? You're talking to the king of the comic books." He threw his hands up triumphantly, getting so loud that he startled poor Selina, who went streaking out of the room, her claws skittering across the tiles. "The Evanston Public Library superhero quiz bowl champion, three years running. A feat never accomplished before or since! Hip-hip huzzah!"

I snatched the whipped cream out of his hand. "They had comic books when you were a kid?" I knew they did. I'd seen his collection. But for some reason, I wanted to change the subject.

My dad rolled his eyes. "Naturally. But they were painted onto cave walls." He ruffled my hair before snatching the canister back and putting it in the fridge. "And every last one of them had a fantastic origin story which shaped the identities of the world's greatest heroes."

Frankly, I was much more interested in the ice cream. "Oh yeah?" I said.

"A tragic one too. Say, the lone survivor of an alien race who falls to earth in the midst of a meteor shower and decides to become a hero." He held up a spoon, slashing it through the air like it was a sword.

"Some kids *thought* she was an alien," I said, drifting out of the kitchen and into the living room.

He followed after me. In the small stretch of hallway between the kitchen and the living room hung a picture of my mother. We both waved to her out of habit. It was a ritual, I guess. I mean, it was a picture. It wasn't like either of us expected her to wave back. But we still did it. Without questioning or considering, or even talking about it, we paid our respects.

It helped not to miss her so much.

Now that I was older, I understood that when my dad said our old house was haunted, he meant by the memory of her. Every room had her fingerprints on it, in one way or another.

Sometimes, though, I felt pretty sure that her ghost had followed us here to the apartment. At least she was a friendly one, even if she sometimes made us sad.

"We would have probably heard about any meteors crashing down in the middle of Deerwood Park, wouldn't we?" Dad continued.

"Probably." News traveled around a small town, after all. Especially in the middle school. I dropped down into my usual spot on the living room floor, between the coffee table and the leather recliner, pulling my legs in and setting the bowl on my lap. We always ate ice cream in front of the TV. *K-911* was our favorite show and it was on tonight. It followed the adventures of real-life police dogs. We knew all of their names and could identify each of them before the scrawl at the bottom of the screen gave it away. Right before each commercial break, the enthusiastic narrator would ask the viewers a multiple-choice question, canine trivia. My dad and I would play along, although he usually beat me.

Okay, he *always* beat me, unless the episode was a rerun. But it didn't matter what happened within our own walls. No gossip would ever reach the world outside.

I reached for the remote, but my dad got it first.

"Maybe she's a mutant."

"A mutant?"

"An ordinary girl who suddenly developed superpowers after being bitten by a radioactive..."—he trailed off, tapping the remote against his chin—"*something*. Do you know what she can do? What are her superpowers?"

It seemed like her greatest superpower was her ability to distract my dad from our night. "I don't know," I said. "She can't sew. I think the big *C* was glued to her cape. Are you going to turn on the—"

"Hmm...this is a tricky one. Clearly, she wasn't bitten by a radioactive sewing machine."

"Dad!"

He sat down on the arm of the sofa. "Come on, come on, come on. I love a good challenge. Tell me what she can do, Janey."

There was no way I was going to get my *K-911* tonight.

"I don't know, Dad," I said, stabbing my spoon into the whipped cream. "She's really good at shouting?"

"Shouting?"

I rolled my eyes. "'Captain Superlative is here to make all troubles disappear!'" I used the air quotes again.

"Catchy. I like it." He slid down onto the couch. "Bitten by a radioactive megaphone?"

"I don't think so."

"Hmm... Captain Superlative..."

We sat in silence, my dad hogging the remote. He kept repeating her name over and over and over again. I shoveled the ice cream into my mouth, watching him from beneath my eyelashes. And I only stopped because I was going to give myself an ice-cream headache. "I don't even know what her name means," I said after a moment.

"A captain is the highest-ranking person on the starship *Enterprise*."

"Dad!"

He chuckled. "What? That wasn't what you were looking for?"

*"Superlative."*

"I see you're paying attention in language-arts class," he said sarcastically. Tyler Jeffries was in that class. *Of course* I wasn't paying attention. I was supposed to be paying attention to him! Drawing his lips in the corner of my book. And I was doing fine anyway. I was pretty sure I had a B-minus.

"A superlative is something excellent, magnificent, above all others, the best of the best." He gave me an assessing look. "Does that sound like Captain Superlative?"

"She's fearless. I'll give her that."

"Aren't all superheroes fearless? I'll have to check my comics, but I think that's part of the job description."

I made a face. "You'd have to be fearless to show up wearing ridiculous clothing like that."

"Ridiculous clothing?"

"A bathing suit and tights."

"Oh my."

"She wasn't even wearing jeans! Or Blue Shoes!"

Blue Shoes were the latest craze. They had been ever since Dagmar came back from summer break wearing the pair that her mother bought for her. Everyone owned a pair. They were bright, plastic blue shoes, the color of a twilight sky, with silver glitter melted into the molding. To tell the truth, they were pretty uncomfortable. They had a thick band that cut across the top of the foot that dug into your ankle. And that wasn't even the worst part. No, the worst came with every step. Accompanying the pain from the band was a squeak, like a dog's worn-out chew toy. The squeak was even worse when the shoes were wet.

I never left home without my pair.

"Good for her," my dad said.

He *would*.

And then, finally, he turned on the TV. I thought that meant the end of it. But as the opening theme song of *K-911* started to play and Selina softly crept into the room, he said, "We'll have to collect more information."

"It was probably just some kind of joke."

"You think so?"

"Yeah. Everything will go back to normal tomorrow."

He ran his hand along the length of my hair. Jealously, Selina hopped up into his lap. He petted her too. "If you say so, Janey."

And we lapsed into the comfortable silence that always came with watching police dogs go running through an obstacle course.

The return to routine lulled me back from the brink of frustration. This was how it was supposed to be. Each day the same as the last, time marching slowly on. It wasn't exciting, but it was safe. It was comfortable. And, in my ignorance, I thought it was right. It had never occurred to me that human beings were born with the innate desire to go faster and forward. I was happy where I was. Why hurtle headlong into the abyss where the future waited?

# 3

**Looking back, I should have known** better. About a great many things, of course, but most of all about Captain Superlative and her ambitions. You can't really go back to normal after being hit by a tsunami. The landscape is never quite the same again. That's just how it works.

But you know what they say about hindsight and all.

When I woke up the next day, I had completely forgotten about Captain Superlative. Maybe I had willfully forgotten about her, determined to have everything go back to the way it was. I don't know. At any rate, she was the farthest thing from my mind that morning.

My dad dropped me off at the circle drive in front of the school, like always. I smiled and waved at him as he drove off, before heading inside. It had snowed a little the night before and the pavement was coated in a thin dusting of flakes, so my Blue Shoes were extra squeaky—everyone's were. The hallways were a symphony of squeaks and squawks.

Paige was one of the few students who moved silently, in her old, beat-up sneakers.

She passed me by, head down, face framed by a curtain of braids with little silver and gold bands around them, carrying her books in her arms, like always. Singled out by silence, she was an easy target to spot. "Nice shoes, Paige," Dagmar said, appearing out of a cluster of girls around the trophy case. She positioned herself directly in Paige's path. Paige tried to veer to one side, but the book on top of her stack slid over. In trying to compensate, shifting in the opposite direction, she overcorrected and lost her balance altogether. Her books came toppling down, landing with a clatter as her shoulder hit the wall.

Dagmar towered over Paige, looking especially pleased. "You know, I think we should send you as a gift to the Kohn soccer team. It would guarantee they never won anything."

The hallway echoed with agreement from the moths.

Just the typical beginning to a typical morning. Dagmar planted her fists on her waist, almost daring Paige to say anything back. But I knew she wouldn't. She never did. Paige's head was ducked low. I noticed that her eyes were fixed on a specific point, on Dagmar's left wrist.

There was a mark there; a fresh bruise, all purple and pink.

It didn't escape Dagmar's attention that Paige was looking. It was only a split second, but I could see it in her hawkish eyes. I thought she might say something, but one of the girls from the group of moths called out, "Come *on*, Dagmar.

You said you'd help me with my math homework." Dagmar let out a huff and bumped Paige's arm as she blazed by. Not hard enough to hurt Paige. It was just a warning. That Dagmar *could* hurt her.

Like that, it was over.

Dagmar walked off—probably to *do* her friend's homework for her, given how protective she was of the soccer team. Paige rubbed the side of her arm. She glanced around, her eyes gazing at me and a few others before she knelt down to start collecting her books and papers, now damp with melted and dirty snow. The warning bell rang, picking up the pace of the hallway's ebb and flow. Kids swirled past Paige in a flurry of squeaky shoes and self-absorbed importance. Someone kicked one of her books. Someone else stepped on her math worksheet. Another crunched down on her pencil. Her graphing calculator skidded into the wall, causing the little flap over the battery compartment to pop open.

Somehow, the word *ostracism* crept back into my mind.

Oddball.

Outlander.

Outsider.

Outcast.

I was about to turn away and head off to class, thinking nothing more of the encounter, when the hallway began to thunder with the sound of stomping, racing feet going faster than the code of conduct would allow.

"Hellooooooooo, citizen!"

Captain Superlative appeared, rushing down the hall like the waters of a flash flood, her arms held up and her fingers straight and tightly pressed together to slice through the air as she flew.

She was back. It twisted my stomach a little to see her in all of her kitchen-gloved glory. She stood out in all the wrong ways. And she was unapologetic about it.

What kind of person would do that?

Captain Superlative zipped to Paige, kids jumping out of her way. "It looks like you could use some help!"

Flustered, Paige looked up. "Well, I..."

She didn't seem to know how to finish her sentence. But it didn't seem to matter all that much. Suddenly Captain Superlative was down on her hands and knees, sweeping up Paige's books. A few kids stopped to watch with me. Including Tyler Jeffries. The corner of his lip curled up. I wondered what he was thinking, and I stared at him until he turned to catch my eye. I shyly looked back at the scene.

Captain Superlative offered Paige her neatly stacked things. "There you go, citizen! And don't lose this one." She tapped the fingertips of her glove on a sheet of lined paper at the top of the pile, covered in Paige's scrawling handwriting. "It's a new song, isn't it?"

*Song?*

"Yeah," Paige said, accepting the stack like some kind of a gift, instead of her schoolwork. "It...is. It's not finished yet. I just...can't think of a good title."

"Well, what's it about?"

"It's for my brother, Tyrone. It's about his little cars and how he has to clean them up when he's done playing."

"Matchbox Madness," I thought silently. Or "Hot Wheels Havoc."

"If it's for your brother, why don't you name it after him? That way he'll know that it's special!" Captain Superlative said. "How about 'Tyrone's Toys'?"

A slow smile crept over Paige's face. "Yeah," she said. "Yeah, I think I like that. Thank you!"

"No need, citizen! That's what Captain Superlative is here to do!"

"I'm—"

"Paige McCoy!" Captain Superlative interrupted, grinning fiercely. "I know who you are!"

And with that, she raised her arms and flew away again.

Those of us watching—at least a dozen kids—didn't seem quite sure what to do. It felt like a play that had ended suddenly—no curtain call, no round of applause. Just a quick stop that left us all with whiplash and confusion. Tyler was the one who came back to life first. "Huh," he said, glancing over at one of his friends with that crooked little smile. "How about that?"

"Jealous someone's hogging the spotlight, great one?" the friend asked, giving Tyler a dramatic bow.

Tyler shook his head. "Nah. I think she's cool."

The hallway immediately echoed with girls agreeing:

"Cool."

"Yeah, cool."

"Totally cool."

The second bell rang. Life resumed. I was the only one who remained frozen, watching the scene play out again in my mind amid the swirling of the dust. For a moment, I felt a shiver run through me. Like when I was little and my dad would tease me, dropping ice cubes down the back of my collar during our family trips to the park. My body actually shook. I grabbed the charm on my necklace. *So she'd picked up Paige's things and known her name. That was no big deal. Anyone could do that.*

And yet... Tyler Jeffries called it cool.

That made her worth noticing, didn't it?

The day seemed, in many ways, like any other day. In social studies, Ms. Hinton talked about the ancient Greeks and their habits—applauding to silence something they didn't like, playing throwing games with the dregs of their drinks, burning bones as offerings to gods they didn't actually believe in—and praising Dagmar for her insightful questions. I passed through language-arts class staring at Tyler Jeffries, along with every other girl in the class. We ran laps in gym, slowing to a walk when Coach McCullough's back was turned and our sides ached. The creations we turned out in shop class were horrible and lopsided. Things smelled bad in science lab.

But it wasn't like any other day.

The changes were subtle. You could only really notice them in the spaces in between, in the hallways, in the passing periods when life was organized chaos and we were free from the watchful eyes of our teachers.

I was at my locker, getting my math homework. There was a little mirror on the inside of the door, a giveaway my dad had gotten at a veterinary conference, with print that read *Vetoquinol Laxatone: For Cats with Hairballs* in the lower right-hand corner. I stopped to look at myself—nothing special, just a typical girl with typical brown hair and typical brown eyes. Completely normal.

Natural.

Neutral.

Nonentity.

Over my shoulder, I noticed another typical girl like me. I'd never seen her before. New kid. Probably fresh from the fort.

Her forehead was furrowed up as she stared fixedly at the school map in her hands. Lost, I figured. The school was kind of confusing. The running joke was that the architects had built it with eight different wings branching out from the front entrance, in the shape of an octopus, because it rained so often. They wanted the school to be able to swim if Deerwood Park ever flooded.

I heard Captain Superlative before I saw her, accompanied by the pounding of her sneakers, arms raised as if her small body was flying again. She rushed over to the new girl's side, coming to a stop with her hands on her hips. "You look like you're in need of a rescue, citizen!"

The girl clearly didn't know what to make of Captain Superlative. It probably wasn't the kind of new-school welcome she was used to getting. She opened and closed her mouth a few times, like a goldfish. "Um . . . I . . . uh . . . looking for the cafeteria?" she said.

Captain Superlative beamed at her, putting a hand on her shoulder and turning her to face the other way. "Second door to the right, citizen!"

I frowned a little. I'd kind of figured that Captain Superlative *had* to be a new kid too. But now I wasn't so sure. She knew Paige's name and she knew her way around the school, as if she'd been here forever.

"Thanks," the girl said, smiling. "My name's Nicole."

"Nice to meet you, Nicole."

"You too, uh . . . ?"

"Captain Superlative!"

"Captain Superlative."

"Have a great lunch! It's taco day!" Captain Superlative said, giving the girl's shoulder a squeeze.

The girl headed down the hall. She paused once, glancing over her shoulder to wave at Captain Superlative, then continued, disappearing into the cafeteria. There was the slightest bounce in her step.

Captain Superlative turned again. For a second, I thought she could see me watching her reflection. She looked like she was about to say something else, but the bell rang.

Raising her arms, she flew off.

It was after my lunch period that I caught my next glimpse of Captain Superlative. I was taking my tray to the garbage can. The tacos at our school were not that impressive. My dad's were better and I was thinking that I'd probably ask him to make them for dinner. My lunch was more or less untouched. I had convinced myself the meat was cat food. As I tossed it, I saw Kevin Marks leaving the cafeteria. Kevin was one of Tyler's friends. He'd been cast to play Cogsworth in *Beauty and the Beast* until he broke his femur while goofing off on the auditorium stage, back in November. The recovery had been slow. He was in a wheelchair now and still not quite used to it.

He rolled up to the glass cafeteria doors. Normally, they were propped open, but someone had kicked the doorstop and they were shut. There was a large metal button beside them that was supposed to make them swing open automatically. He tried to wheel up as close to the button as he could, reaching out to push it. But he couldn't reach. The angle of his wheels left him just an inch too far back. His fingertips could just barely brush against the metal, his face turning pink from the effort. He tried a few different arrangements, clumsily fumbling with his wheelchair, catching his fingers in the spokes as he struggled to figure it out.

From out of nowhere, Captain Superlative came racing to the other side of the door. "Right this way, citizen," she said, pulling it open, gesturing grandly for Kevin to pass.

"Puzzled" couldn't begin to describe the look on his face. Kevin's jaw just hung open a moment or two before he snapped it shut. "Thanks," he finally said, stuttering a little bit.

As he wheeled himself through the door, Captain Superlative reached behind him and grabbed one of the handles with her free hand to help expertly guide the chair as it turned. "Have a good day, Kevin!" she said. "May no more villainous doors get in your way!"

Decisively, she kicked the doorstop back into place, giving it a firm nod, as if to say, *Ha! So there!*

Several kids in the hall stopped to watch Captain Superlative. It gave me another shudder, just seeing it. But she smiled and waved before taking off in the opposite direction. Better her than me, I supposed. I'd die from some of the looks of confusion she was getting.

By the end of the day, everyone had a Captain Superlative story or two. I caught snatches of conversation as I drifted along:

"Did you hear? She wore the costume in *class*!"

"No!"

"I know. It's totally against the dress code."

"Ms. Esrick even called her Captain Superlative."

"You're kidding."

"Nope! She said, 'Thanks for helping Mitchell with his assignment, Captain Superlative.'"

"It can't possibly say that on the class list."

"The teachers are in on it."

"It's got to be Rachael, right? She's still upset about not getting to play Belle."

"No, Rachael's family just shipped out."

"Huh."

"And Captain Superlative helped Claudia with her vocab worksheet. You *know* how much Rachael hated Claudia."

Before my last period, I spotted her one more time. It was definitely the weirdest incident yet. By then, I'd started looking out for her whenever someone dropped something or needed help. Like a game. No one seemed to be in need, though, so she caught me completely by surprise.

We were lined up outside of the auditorium, where we took Drama, my least favorite class and one I definitely wouldn't have taken if it weren't required. I was in the class with Dagmar. And April, of course. Anywhere Dagmar went, April followed. She'd been that way back when we were friends too. It was like she just couldn't exist alone. The two of them were whispering behind their hands just ahead of me in line. Dagmar had her cell phone out. The light of the screen splashed over her face, giving her a greenish-yellow glow. I could have listened to them if I'd wanted to. But I'd heard it all before.

And then Captain Superlative sidled up to Dagmar without warning.

"Helloooooooo, Dagmar!"

Half surprised, half mortified, Dagmar turned around to face her, clumsily hiding her phone behind her back. Everyone stopped and watched.

Dagmar's expression cooled. She put on the face of someone who could not be rattled, someone who was above everything. Her eyes flicked up and down, the way they usually did when she was looking for a target. Dagmar had a knack for finding one little flaw or imperfection on a person and blowing it wildly out of proportion until it became who you were. You had a zit and you were Pizza Face for the rest of your life. You were too tall and she miraculously always managed to cut your head out of frame when taking a group picture. A stuffy nose and you were suddenly Stuffy the Clown. But what could she say about someone who was so openly peculiar, literally wearing her otherness like a uniform? Nothing, it seemed. "What do you want?" she asked lazily, playing with a piece of her golden hair when she came up empty.

Captain Superlative smiled at her. The top part of the mask shifted up a little, so I could tell that the smile went all the way to her eyes. "I just wanted to let you know that you're looking very pretty today!"

This was followed by another one of those dead silences that Captain Superlative was quickly becoming very good at creating.

I had to admit, though, she was right. Dagmar was wearing her hair up in a high ponytail with curls cascading down her shoulders like lava. She had on a very bold, very stylish red sweater and designer jeans, the kind she wore when she wasn't in her soccer uniform. Plus her Blue Shoes. Everything about her was flawless.

Faultless.

Fanciful.

Fantastic.

Except for that bruise on her wrist, which, I noticed with a little surprise, she'd tried to cover up with some makeup.

"What?" Dagmar's snappish tone of voice was less glamorous than her appearance.

"That sweater, it really brings out the color of your eyes," Captain Superlative said cheerfully.

There was no way to even guess how Dagmar would respond. I'm not sure she even knew how, but she was spared by the sound of the bell.

Like always, Captain Superlative raised her arms over her head and prepared to take flight. "Time for gym class! More people to save! Captain Superlative is here to make all troubles disappear!"

And she was gone.

The door to the auditorium opened. We started to file inside.

"I can't stand her," Dagmar said in a low hiss, a voice only meant to be heard by April.

"I know," April said, ever the loyal sidekick.

Dagmar slipped her phone into her back pocket, pulling down her sweater to hide it with expert precision. "All day today, it's been nothing but 'Captain Superlative this' and 'Captain Superlative that.'"

"I guess."

"She's all anyone can talk about! Her and her stupid baked-potato outfit."

"Don't worry about it," April said. "It's almost the Valentine's Day dance. You'll be queen and all anyone can talk about. Just like last year."

Tyler Jeffries was walking down the hall, going the other way. Every single girl in the line stopped to watch him go, much to the annoyance of all the boys who were bumped and jostled in the process. "Hey," Tyler said, smiling.

"Hey, Ty," one of the boys said. "I'm performing today. What's your advice, Shakespeare?"

"Be a better actor," Tyler replied cheerfully. "Pretend you're me."

A couple of the boys laughed.

"But alas," Tyler said, touching the back of his hand to his forehead. "There can be but one with talent such as mine."

Someone threw a crumpled-up piece of paper at him.

"I am a gift to the stage!"

All the boys groaned.

"Break a leg," he called to his friend, laughing and waving as he continued down the hall.

I wasn't sure who he was waving to. Dagmar seemed convinced it was her, though. "Tyler is so going to ask me to the dance," she said, leaning back over her shoulder to April. "You can see it in his eyes."

April laughed, nodding eagerly. "Totally."

Dagmar shook her head and started walking again, which meant that all the other girls started walking again. "I hope Captain *Freak* doesn't ruin it."

"Nah, she doesn't seem interested in Tyler." Sacrilege, if I ever heard it. "And I don't think she wants to be Valentine's Day queen, Dagmar," April continued. "Even if she wanted to be, what would anyone write on the ballot? 'Captain Superlative'? That's not a real name."

"That's what all the teachers are calling her."

"Yeah, I know."

"Not the point, April."

"Don't worry about it, Dagmar. It won't last. She'll get bored. I mean, it can't possibly be fun making study guides for social-studies tests or opening doors for random strangers."

"Study guides?"

April reached into her messenger bag, slung over her right hip. She pulled out a packet of papers, bound with a bright red staple in the top left-hand corner. "She made them for everyone in Ms. Hinton's sixth-period class. To study for that big test. And she told us to hang on to the staple because—you'll love this—*red is a lucky color.*"

Dagmar took the papers from April, violently crumpling them up and throwing them on the ground. "She is such a *freak*!"

April shrugged.

"Dagmar." Mr. Hoffman, our drama teacher, appeared at the door. He was a tall, lanky man with salt-and-pepper hair that was swept back off his forehead. "Looking forward to your monologue today," he said, bending over at the waist, offering her that Dagmar-special smile.

She flashed him a grin. "I've been working superhard on it."

"Excellent."

Dagmar and April disappeared into the auditorium. I followed after them, scooping up the study guide from the floor. Across the top, I could see the words *Ancient Greece.* Not only was Captain Superlative not a new kid, she was in my grade. She had Ms. Hinton, who only taught seventh graders. I unfolded the packet, smoothing it out between my hands. The first section was about ostracism, about how the Greeks voted politically dangerous citizens into exile.

No question in my mind who Dagmar would ostracize now. There was something about Captain Superlative that was dangerous.

Deviant.

Disastrous.

Deadly.

# 4

**The incident in the hallway—really,** the whole day—left me feeling strangely uncomfortable in my own skin. I found myself constantly digging my fingernails into my arm or my knee, and chewing on the inside of my cheek and lower lip. It felt like my blood had been replaced by pop fizzing through my veins. I was buzzing. I was out of place, out of sync with the way things were supposed to go, and I wanted to strip off the feeling. I wanted to tear it away from me like a rumpled old sweater that I could toss into a corner and forget. But it was a part of me. And I couldn't tear away a piece of me.

I didn't like it.

It was irritating and distracting and made doing my homework impossible. Words blurred before me, and I found myself drawing Captain Superlative's cape all over my notebooks instead of answering questions about the ancient Greeks. It was only when my dad and I began our nightly rituals that I started to come back to myself. I slipped back into comfortable familiarity, sitting in my usual spot on the floor of the living room after a usual dinner and usual ice cream.

The ice cream and episode of *K-911* were followed up by our weekly coupon clipping. My dad and I crawled through the pages of the local newspapers, each with our own list of items to find. Laundry detergent. Mouthwash. Spaghetti sauce and string cheese. All the ingredients for my dad's triple-fudge-chunk brownies. Whoever found the most coupons in thirty minutes, before the news ended, won.

Again, usually my dad—who read much faster than I could—won the game.

The so-very-serious anchorwoman on the TV was talking about a wanted criminal who'd just been caught in Chicago. My dad glanced up at the mug shot, the guy with a gold tooth and a tattoo over his right eye standing there with a card in front of his chest, snarling at the camera. "Ha," he said. And again, louder. "Ha."

It was a strange noise, one that startled Selina, who leaped off her perch above the window and landed on the arm of the recliner. Not his usual laugh. I looked up from a coupon for powdered sugar. "What?"

"I was just thinking about what you told me. About your day."

"About Captain Superlative."

*What else?*

"Maybe it'll be her picture on the screen next," he said. "I mean, opening doors for classmates? Showing new students around the school? Her reign of terror has to end. Call in Scotland Yard."

"Scotland what?"

"The British police."

I rolled my eyes. "You don't understand."

"If parents had dimes for every time they were told that they didn't understand, we'd all be millionaires and then I could pay someone to understand for me and I could take a vacation to Australia."

"Bring me back a koala." I went back to cutting the coupon. "She isn't a . . ." I couldn't find the right word. "She's just different."

"Everyone is different," he said, riffling through a few pages of his newspaper. "If we were all the same, we'd all be named Bob and we'd all like country music." He curled his upper lip. "'My truck done left me and my woman broke down,'" he said with a horrible, fake Southern accent.

"I mean *different* different. Weird."

He shrugged. "There's nothing wrong with being a little weird. Weird people teach us what it is we value most. When you go 'that's weird,' what you're really saying is such-and-such is what I like best."

Of course he'd say something like that. I sighed softly. "It's okay to be a *little* weird, but this is too much."

He made a soft popping noise with his mouth, setting down his scissors. Was he forfeiting? We still had five minutes to go on the news. Seemed so, as he reached over for the remote, turning off the TV. "Any idea what her secret identity could be?" he asked me.

"Secret identity?"

"All superheroes have them. What? Do you think they sleep in their superhero costumes? They wear pj's just the same as the rest of us."

He stood up, crossing the living room. Compared to our old house, it was cramped with just the couch and recliner, the glass coffee table, the TV mounted on the wall, and a couple of bookcases. They weren't exactly bookcases, though. They were more like trophy cases, displaying our most valued possessions: Dad's college diploma in a gold frame, the ink prints of my feet from the hospital when I was born, a picture of my parents from their wedding, my winning nighttime landscape from the third-grade art fair, and some of my dad's most prized comic books. I once asked him what made them more special than the others on the shelf in his bedroom. He said something about limited-edition collector's items and that they would put my grandkids through college.

He picked up one of the comic books, handling it like a newborn kitten. He opened the cover, thumbing through the pages until he found what he was looking for and turned it for me to see. On one panel, an ordinary-looking man in a gray suit and tie with glasses. On the next panel, a ridiculous superhero in a ridiculous getup—a dark blue leotard with a pattern of white stars along one side and a flowing white cape—soaring through the sky with his fingers held the same ridiculous way that Captain Superlative held hers. Two people in one.

*"Da-ad,"* I said, my voice rising into a little bit of a whine. "We're supposed to be playing coupons."

"This game is much more fun!"

I slapped my scissors down on the table and flopped back

against the recliner, folding my arms across my chest. Selina let out a yelp and jumped up from the chair, scampering out of the room.

"Scaredy-cat," my dad called after her, before turning back to me. "What do you know about Captain Superlative?"

"Really?"

"Come on!"

"I know she's in my grade," I said with a sigh. "She has Ms. Hinton for social studies."

"Her and one hundred and fifty other kids."

"And she's not a fort kid."

"Well, that's a good start. I'll make a detective out of you yet. Noticed anyone missing from your classes lately?" he asked, taking a seat in the recliner. His fingers brushed against my hair. "Someone who might be running around with a big *C* on her back?"

"Not really."

"You're kidding me."

"Our seats all got reassigned after winter break. And anyway, the teachers are all in on it."

"What do you mean?"

"Even *they're* calling her Captain Superlative."

"Interesting... She really is a superhero, then," my dad said, a slight chuckle in his voice. "A superhero's secret identity is always someone entirely ordinary. Someone anonymous, who you wouldn't notice. Someone you would never suspect of being superlative."

Paige, Dagmar, April, Tyler. Half of Dagmar's friends. Yeah. If any of them were suddenly replaced by someone in tights and a cape, kids would notice. But as I thought about all of my classes and my classmates, I saw a lot of blank faces. They blended into one another, vanishing. If one of them disappeared, I wouldn't know it. "That's half the class."

"Half the class?"

I shrugged, settling back against the side of the recliner. "It's better to be that way, I think. Unknown. Anonymous."

"Why?"

"You don't get burned by Dagmar Hagen, for one thing." If Paige ever disappeared, everyone would be tripping over one another, fleeing from the possibility of becoming Dagmar's new target.

I'd be right there with them.

My dad sighed. "Ah yes. The big *D*."

He tapped his ear. The word came to me easily. "Dominating."

"Demanding."

"Diva."

"Dreadful."

I couldn't argue with that. She was dreadful. "Yeah," I said, conceding the point to him.

He set the comic book down on the coffee table, leaning forward in the seat and bowing his head so that he could look at me, partly upside down. "Is that how you like to be seen, Janey?" he asked.

"What?"

"Anonymous. Just a regular old face in the crowd?"

I blinked in surprise at the question. "Well, yeah."

"Just Plain Jane?"

"Yes."

"Well," he said, "I'm very glad that I don't get Plain Jane at home."

"Who do you get here?"

"Here, I get Janey. With an exclamation point. I get *Janey!*"

"Same thing."

"Absolutely not. My *Janey!* is funny, interesting, witty. Nothing plain about her at all."

Plain Jane wasn't so bad, I thought. I'd been called worse, anyway. For a week, when I was nine, I'd been "the girl whose mother died." That had been miserable. "You don't know what it's like, Dad."

"Don't I?"

"No."

For some reason, that made him laugh. "Blissful ignorance! Achieved at last! My life is complete."

"Dad!" I laughed too, in spite of myself. "Stop being weird."

"I happen to enjoy being weird."

"How are we related?"

"Only by blood, Janey." He slid off the end of the recliner, folding up his long legs so that he could sit on the floor, squeezed between the recliner and the table, next to me. It was a tight fit. A funny fit. But his closeness always meant something to me. It made me think of the days, back in the house, when I'd wake up in the middle of the night, dreaming of giant monsters that gobbled up people. He'd come into my room, sit on the side of my bed, and stroke my hair until I fell back asleep. That always did the trick. Like magic.

Like a superpower.

"Plain Jane doesn't make a lot of friends," he said.

This was an old argument. Most parents longed for quiet, low-maintenance kids who never strayed from the path or broke the speed limit. My dad probably would have jumped for joy if I ever threw a party and trashed the apartment. "I'm fine, Dad," I told him for the millionth time. "I like being a loner. It gives me . . ."

"Mystique?"

"Yeah." Whatever that meant.

"Are you really so scared of someone like Dagmar Hagen disliking you that you'd rather be nothing more than a face in the crowd?" he asked.

"It's better than getting picked on."

"Is it?"

I closed my eyes, replaying scenes where she showed her temper. The time she'd kicked Paige's towel into the pool during summer camp. The time she'd made fun of Paige's jeans until she cried. The time she'd thrown Paige's training bra into the boys' locker room. "She's brutal, Dad."

"Then why isn't she in detention where she belongs?"

"You try telling the teachers that the service-award-winning star of the soccer team is secretly a monster."

"The way you talk, the other kids should be lining up to tell the teachers that."

"And risk the team falling apart? Nuh-uh. Not going to happen. They're going to go all the way this year. Crushing Kohn."

"Uh-huh . . ."

"Besides, who else would show them the latest Joshua Goldman music video?" Or whatever.

"Yes. Where would we be without music videos?"

The scenes continued to play themselves out. The time Dagmar berated two girls for sitting with Paige at lunch. The time she'd compared Paige's hair to a mop head. What was it about Paige? Was it that she looked like an easy target, with her delicate, birdlike limbs and secondhand clothes? Or was there more to it? I'd never really thought about it before.

"Believe me, Dad," I said. "I've seen it. I just don't want to get burned."

"I see."

But I didn't think he saw. People always said "I see" when they didn't really see at all. There was no way he could understand.

He wrapped an arm around me, his thumb brushing against the side of my shoulder. "Is Captain Superlative getting picked on?"

"You should hear the things everyone is saying about her."

The scene outside of the auditorium played out again:

*"She is such a freak!"*

Dagmar said it with such poison in her voice, such fury, that for a second, she didn't look like a rising pop sensation so much as a demon. *Freak* wasn't just a word. It was a curse. Not like a cuss that would get you sent to the principal's office (not that any teacher would believe Dagmar Hagen capable of swearing), but a spell that would derail the course of your destiny. There was nothing worse you could be called, nothing that made it clearer that you didn't belong. Every school had the popular girls and the losers and the jocks and the smart kids and the theatre kids. But freaks? They weren't a part of the social construct. They just didn't belong.

"I'll tell you one thing."

My dad's voice broke through the flashback. I opened my eyes, looking at him. "What?"

"If I were in your place," he said, staring at the comic book on the coffee table, "I'd really like to know more about this Captain Superlative."

He'd made that clear enough with all of his questions. But I just didn't understand. "It's just so—"

"Weird?"

"Weird. With a capital *W*."

He touched his ear. "Wild."

"Wacky."

"Willful."

"Wrong."

"Wonderful."

I faltered. "Wonderful?"

Repeating a word meant you lost. My dad gave me a triumphant little smile before standing up. His knees cracked. Once again he brushed his fingers against my hair. And then he started gathering up the coupons and newspapers. He wasn't even counting to see who'd won. He just piled them all up and folded them into his pocket before grabbing the excess cuttings and carrying them out of the room and down the hall to be recycled.

I reached across the table, grabbing the pad of paper with the shopping list. I turned it to a new page and started to draw. Captain Superlative appeared, shooting through the sky. I added stars and comets and spinning planets with dozens of twirling moons. A blazing sun with dark spots and flares. The ballet of the universe. It was quite the picture. She was traveling faster than the speed of light, zooming from one galaxy to the next. She was—

It was so ridiculous!

I slapped the pad and pencil down on the table, shoving them away from me. Captain Superlative wasn't about to go flying through the universe. She was just a girl. Just a *normal* girl. Somehow. Under all of that costuming.

I stared accusingly at the comic book. It was strange to feel angry at a few sheets of paper, but it kept giving my dad all these ideas. More upsettingly, my dad was giving me ideas.

# 5

**The bruise on Dagmar's wrist was** turning yellowy by the end of the week. But I noticed there was another, a little bit higher up on her arm. It looked like a centipede, a misshapen, short centipede made of small circles. I saw it as she was walking through the hall before homeroom Thursday morning, when her sleeve shifted for a second or two. She was pinning up a sign on one of the bulletin boards, part of her campaign for Valentine's Day queen. Only Dagmar would start campaigning a month early for a vote that meant nothing and would already go to her anyway.

DAGMAR HAGEN TAKES THE BACON!

The slogan was a stretch, but I guess she couldn't think of anything else that rhymed with *Hagen*.

*Shaken?* I thought. Or *taken* or *awaken* or *mistaken*?

She stepped back from the sign, furtively glancing from side to side, before sneaking her cell phone out to snap a picture of the bulletin board. My guess was that the precaution was more for show. She wanted to draw attention to the fact that she was flouting the rules. And it worked. It worked deliciously well. Other kids passing by nodded their heads toward her, exchanged winks back and forth, all suppressing giggles and smirks.

"Posting that?" someone asked her.

"You bet," she replied. She held up two fingers, drawing the lines of an invisible hashtag in the air. "#QueenDagmar."

"Nice!"

Dagmar hid her phone just as Ms. Hinton came passing through with a stack of three-ring binders. "Cute sign, Dagmar."

"Thanks, Ms. Hinton!" Dagmar said pleasantly, giving her a smile. "Oh! And my mom says hi."

"How's she doing?"

"Great!"

"Tell her to come back and visit sometime. Everyone in the teachers' lounge is dying to see her."

"I will."

"Thank you, Dagmar. I'll see you in class."

How anyone could go from being sugary-sweet one moment to dangerous the next without being exhausted all the time was beyond me. But experience in dodging Dagmar's wrath had taught me to spot signs of the change. In this case, the transformation came silently, in the form of Paige with her bundle of books and her soft-soled sneakers. She turned a corner, passed Ms. Hinton, and froze.

Was it Dagmar's perfume or her shining curls that alerted Paige? No way to know for sure. I could see Paige's dark eyes dart from point to point, looking for a possible escape. But before she could make up her mind on the best course of action, Dagmar saw her.

In a blink, Dagmar swept in beside her, one palm planted firmly on the wall, subtly blocking her from going forward. "Hey, Paige."

No one would have taken that for a kind greeting. And Paige didn't. "Dagmar," she said, her voice tired, her neck and shoulders hunching, like she was trying to hide behind her hair.

Dagmar's lovely green eyes flicked down to Paige's shoes, then back up. Target acquired. She had a perfectly feigned expression of surprise. "So where *are* your Blue Shoes, anyway?" she asked sweetly, as though she didn't know Paige never wore them.

"I don't have any."

"Oh yeah. That's right. I forgot." She wound up and struck. "Your dad hasn't had a job in, like, two years." The corners of her lips twitched. "He's a hobo or something, right?"

Emotion flickered across Paige's face, from surprise to pain to exhaustion. Shoulders slumping, head drooping, she sighed an exasperated, little sigh. "Can I go?" she asked. "Please?"

"I forgot!" Dagmar bounced the heel of her palm against the side of her head. "He's in the circus!"

"What?"

"Yeah! I found a picture of him online." She whipped the phone out, punching in a few commands I couldn't see. "It was under the hashtag 'loser.'"

She turned the phone so Paige could see. Trotting along on the screen was a cartoon vagrant clown, with green curls, heavy, gray bags beneath his eyes, and oversize overalls that sagged beneath his flabby arms, with mismatched sleeves. On top of his head, he wore a too-small hat, with a single wilting daisy drooping over one side. With every bouncy step, his long red shoes wobbled like diving boards.

Paige bit her lips together, taking a sharp breath that she let out in an audible exhale. "That's not. My dad." Her tone was crisp. Nearly trembling.

"Really?" Dagmar glanced at the phone again. "Because I can see the resemblance. And look. He's even got a little backpack. Just like your hobo dad." She shook her head, putting the phone away. "It must really hurt," she said. "Not having the money for shoes because your dad is a hobo loser. You must feel awful. So lost. So hopelessly out of place."

"We *have* money for shoes," Paige said.

Obviously. She was wearing them.

Dagmar snorted. "Yeah, sure. Just not *good* ones."

Not the best comeback.

Paige was unfazed. Just tired. "Are we done here?"

"When I say so," Dagmar replied.

"Sometime before that bruise heals up?" Paige said, just under her breath.

I felt a cringe, starting in my forehead and going all the way down to my toes. Briefly, I considered crawling into my locker and praying that there was a secret portal behind it that would whisk me away to a beautiful magical world. Or, really, anywhere that wasn't here.

I doubted I had such luck, of course.

Behind me, Dagmar said, "What was that?"

Paige looked up at her from under her hair. "I said, 'That bruise sure matches your eye shadow.'"

She had rattled Dagmar. Maybe because Paige dared to speak back, or maybe because Paige had managed to strike a blow aimed right at Dagmar's pretty and perfect skin. No one *ever* made fun of the bruises. If anything, most kids secretly admired them. She was the best soccer player in the history of the school. And she had the marks to prove it. Like badges of honor, pinned to a soldier. Each one was a sign of yet another terrific save or daring offensive play. But Dagmar bristled, the tips of her ears turning a little pink. And then her voice went down into a low hiss, like steam escaping from a kettle.

"*You're nothing.* I mean, I don't know how I'd be able to come to school every day if I were you," she said. "I'd just want to curl up and die." Dagmar looked especially pleased with that one.

It was brutal. I felt my jaw drop a little bit. I had to wrap my fingers around the star of my necklace to steady myself, like I'd been dealt a physical blow. It was one thing to make fun of someone's shoes. But to suggest that she'd want to die?

Where had *that* come from?

"Please," Paige said.

"You can go," Dagmar told her.

Dagmar started to move, pulling herself away from the

wall, gesturing for Paige to pass. Paige took a step, then Dagmar slammed her hand back into place, blocking Paige again with a vicious sneer. The DAGMAR HAGEN TAKES THE BACON! poster fell off the board, floating down to earth under the rattle of thumbtacks.

"Not yet."

"But you said—"

"You can go . . . after you look up at me and say, 'I'm a pathetic loser.'"

"What?"

"Do it." Out came the phone once more, a little light flashing at the top. "Say, 'I'm a pathetic loser.' Right into the camera."

Paige looked straight up, into the recording light. "You're a pathetic loser."

"How dare you!"

Dagmar's entire body shook. I didn't know that people were actually capable of shaking with rage. She seemed more like a cartoon character than a person. But Paige couldn't forget that Dagmar was a person. A person with furious heat radiating off of her skin.

Paige looked away, at a couple of kids who were passing down the hall. Both of them turned their heads, pretending to read one of the Valentine's Day dance posters. Her eyes briefly caught mine. She was pleading with me, but I didn't know what to do. What could I do? It's not like I could change Dagmar. Dagmar would always be Dagmar. I could only shrug.

With that, Paige sighed and looked back to Dagmar, staring into the camera. "I'm a—"

"Captain Superlative is here to make all troubles disappear!"

The call came from behind me, at the end of the hall. Paige, Dagmar, and I whipped around to see her. She was standing with her hands on her hips, chin raised at a dramatic angle. The same costume as every day that week, the same tangible confidence that wrapped around her like the cape. Her arms went up and she came zooming down the hall, everyone clearing the way for her. Her cape brushed against me as she ran past, skidding to a stop behind Dagmar's shoulder, putting her palm between Paige and the camera lens.

Dagmar flinched, like she'd just been shocked. Uncomfortably, she stepped away from Paige and the wall, getting out of Captain Superlative's reach. "Not this again," she said with a snarl.

Captain Superlative ignored the venom in her voice, looking instead to Paige. "What seems to be the problem here, citizens?"

"Nothing," Paige replied mildly. "There's no problem."

"She's just in my way," Dagmar said.

Captain Superlative glanced between the two of them. I was sure, even without seeing her face, that she knew just as well as I did that they were both lying. That was what Dagmar and Paige did. "Maybe if you apologized for trying to take a video of her calling herself a pathetic loser, she'd step to one side and let you pass."

"It's okay," Paige said. "I was—"

"You aren't a pathetic loser," Captain Superlative said.

Paige smiled sadly, glancing down over her stack of books

at her feet. "According to popular opinion, I am. I don't have Blue Shoes."

"No, but you *do* write the most beautiful songs for the school choir! And you *are* a straight-A student!"

How did Captain Superlative know any of that about Paige?

"She *wishes*," Dagmar said, looking offended at the very notion of Paige getting good grades.

Captain Superlative ignored her. "And you've been babysitting the Garcia triplets to help your family pay the bills while your dad is looking for a job!"

"Her *loser* dad," Dagmar cut in.

In one sweeping movement, Captain Superlative set herself between Paige and Dagmar, her back to Dagmar, blocking her out. "Your dad is not a loser, Paige," she said firmly. "And neither are you. You're a wonderful person."

The bell rang.

Paige gave a little sigh and turned around, folding her books against her chest as she took off up the hall. I knew I was supposed to do the same. I was going to be late for homeroom, which would mean a warning. Three warnings and it was detention. But I'd never been late before and I couldn't bring myself to look away. There was practically smoke coming out of Dagmar's ears and, as I knew she would, Captain Superlative turned to look at her.

"What is your problem?" Dagmar asked in a low hiss.

"That wasn't very nice," Captain Superlative said. "Is something wrong, Dagmar?"

The question came out of nowhere. What could be wrong if you were Dagmar Hagen? Pretty. Popular. A soccer star.

Top of the class. Destined to be the Valentine's Day queen. She was what we all wanted to be. And, barring that, who we all wanted to be *with*, assuming we were warmed by her flame and not burned by it. Everything was right if you were Dagmar Hagen.

"Wrong?" Dagmar repeated, very softly.

"There has to be a reason you pick on Paige so much," Captain Superlative said.

"Because she's a pathetic loser."

Captain Superlative shook her head. "Only someone who's feeling down would pick on another person. Otherwise, they'd just be evil. And I don't think you're evil, Dagmar."

"I think you're a pain."

"Are you jealous of her?"

"None of your business."

"Maybe you just need a hug."

"Shut up, weirdo."

Much to my surprise—and Dagmar's, I'm sure—Captain Superlative didn't even blink. She spread her arms out, taking a step in, as if to offer Dagmar that hug.

"Stop!" Dagmar held a hand up, and a part of me—clearly the part that spent too much time with my dad's comic books—half expected a fireball to explode out of her palm.

"I just want to be your friend," Captain Superlative said, although she seemed to withdraw.

"Well, I don't want to be your friend," Dagmar replied.

"Why not?"

"Because you're..."

"What?"

"You're just too..."

"Nice?"

*"Freaky!"* Dagmar practically screamed the word. "You're a freak!"

It was the curse again. The one I'd heard outside of the auditorium. A freak. Someone who just didn't belong, someone who had no place in the greater scheme of things. Dagmar had said it to her, not to me, but I shrank back, as if stung.

Captain Superlative did not.

"That doesn't mean we can't be friends," she replied.

I didn't know what to make of that. Neither did Dagmar. She let out an exhausted huff and started down the hall, going out of her way to knock into Captain Superlative's shoulder and throw her off-balance. I could hear her muttering as she went, and decided it was probably a good thing that I couldn't tell what she was saying. Nothing generous, nothing kind.

"You look very pretty in your uniform today!" Captain Superlative called after her, going up on her tiptoes.

"Leave me alone!" Dagmar roared as she turned the corner.

"Good-bye!"

"Shut up!"

"See you later!"

After that, we just listened to the obnoxious squeaking of her Blue Shoes until it faded.

*We* listened.

It was when I could no longer hear Dagmar that I realized the hallway was deserted. It was just the two of us, Captain Superlative and me.

She turned to me. I'd never noticed the fact that the eyeholes of her mask were a little lopsided. Not until they consumed me. She wasn't just looking at me, she was positively *staring* at me. Reading me. Assessing me. Measuring me.

After a moment that was both the longest and the shortest of my life, she leaned over and picked up Dagmar's campaign poster and pinned it back on the board. She raised her arms up over her head. There was no audience to speak of, but she still shouted, "Captain Superlative is here to make all troubles disappear!"

The rest of that afternoon, Dagmar was smoldering. All of us, even April, went out of our way to avoid her. Everyone was sure that getting too close would be like throwing gasoline on the fire. And what made it ten times worse was the reports we got about Captain Superlative's antics. The rest of the day, in addition to her cry of "Captain Superlative is here to make all troubles disappear!" she said, "And don't forget to vote for Dagmar for Valentine's Day queen!"

The incident vibrated through the school and it vibrated through me. But it wasn't Paige's resignation or Dagmar's wrath. It was Captain Superlative. It was how she'd known so much about Paige. It was her questions to Dagmar. How she was rallying support for Dagmar's cause in spite of it all. And it was the way she'd looked at me, like she was seeing something there.

Who did that?

Who was she?

# 6

**Something unexpected happened that** afternoon, after the final bell. Something I couldn't really recall ever happening before. It was me. I jumped out of my seat and shot into the hallway, as if I had somewhere to go or somewhere to be. I was still vibrating from what happened with Dagmar, Paige, and Captain Superlative. Reeling uncontrollably like a dilapidated wagon rolling down a hill. I guess that energy needed to go somewhere. The only trouble was, I wasn't sure which direction it was taking me.

Forward?

I couldn't really tell.

Make no mistake. I wasn't thinking. I was just . . . going. Doing. I was letting that feeling take control of me.

I guess—although I never would have admitted it to myself—I knew deep down that I was looking for *her*. That some instinct was pushing me, driving me toward her and toward—I hoped—the answers to the questions that were bubbling up inside of me.

But, of course, when I finally found her by the front entrance to the school, I panicked. I didn't know why, but as I rounded the corner and spotted the cape, the wig, and the shining swimsuit, my breath caught in my throat and I turned back again, pressing against the wall like I was hiding from the law. Very, very slowly, very, very tentatively, I turned my head to the side, leaning forward to see around to the atrium. It was a small area, watched over by the main office. There were two sets of double doors in front, surrounded by wide windows, decorated with snowflakes and figure skates.

Captain Superlative was holding one of the doors open as Kevin Marks rolled out. "This way, my lord!" she called, with a gloriously awful English accent. She closed it once he was gone, opening it again to let that new girl (Nicole?) pass. "Have a great afternoon, citizen!" Open. Close. Open. Close. When someone came to the door holding a box of supplies, she opened the door. "Wait, wait, wait, I'll get it!" When someone came to the door carrying nothing at all, she opened the door. "There seems to be something blocking your way. Let me take care of that, citizen!" Students. "Bam!" Teachers. "Kapow!" Even the office clerk and the part-time school nurse. "Thwack!" I watched the door and felt the bursts of cool air on my face as she accommodated everyone with an over-the-top greeting and a ridiculously exaggerated effort to open the door.

Soon the school felt abandoned. Everyone who was going home, it seemed, had left. I wondered if Captain Superlative would hang around for a few hours to hold the door open for the soccer team too, once they'd finished their practice. One could only imagine what Dagmar would have to say to that. But as I hid from view, I watched her give the atrium a quick glance; then she ducked out the door herself.

And I followed her.

I don't know where the momentum came from. The part of me that was my dad, maybe? I don't know. Anyone else would have left well enough alone, I think. I just knew that I suddenly had a whirlwind of desire to follow her, to see where she went and what she did and who she was while doing it. I thought that maybe, once we left the school, she'd start to be herself. You know, a normal girl. But as I darted from tree to tree—dark bare branches cutting into a cloudy gray sky—Captain Superlative continued to zoom down the sidewalk with her arms out, the synthetic curls of her wig bouncing against her back. She was flying.

Flaunting.

Fearless.

Free.

The act went on.

There wasn't a lot of town, as far as Deerwood Park was concerned, of course. The school was set on a side street, surrounded by square little houses with white siding and gray rooftops. The end of the block turned into the downtown area. But downtown wasn't much more than a few shops, a gas station, the post office, the ice rink, the movie theater, a burger place (*without* a drive-through), and the train station. The crown jewel of it all was the park: Sunset Ridge Park, a small, grassy area with a few benches, swings, monkey bars, and a slide. After that, nothing but a sea of houses and apartment buildings stretching out to the horizon.

The weather was mild for the middle of January. For us, anyway. Usually, it was icy and cold in Deerwood Park, but this year, it was mostly just wet. The snow had melted, leaving slippery asphalt and dead, muddy grass. It was kind of disgusting. Like a half-finished painting.

I could hear Captain Superlative's footsteps slapping and splashing the ground, which helped me to follow her while keeping out of sight. And for someone running, she didn't seem to be in a great hurry to get anywhere specific. She'd go for a few blocks, then stop to chat with someone, ending the conversation with "Have a good day, citizen!" and then run on. Other times, she would just stop and stare. At a tree. Or the paint peeling off of the side of a house. Or at the ground of the gas station, as if she were admiring the rainbows the sunlight cast in the oil slicks.

We ran past Sunset Ridge, where Tyler Jeffries and some of his friends were tossing a football in the mucky grass, Kevin watching forlornly from the sidelines. "Hey, hey, hey!" Tyler said, running backward with his hands out and open. A boy tossed him the ball and he caught it, starting to dash to some invisible line.

"Go, team!" Captain Superlative shouted at them as she came skidding to a stop. "Good luck, Tyler! I hope you win!"

A couple of the boys laughed and elbowed each other in the ribs, but Tyler turned over his shoulder and smiled, his upper lip stretching out thin. "Thanks!" he said, raising his hand to wave at her.

The other boys all slowly followed suit, waving shyly.

To my surprise, he also waved to me. I did a double take. Well, no. That wasn't possible. He didn't know I existed. But before I could look again, he'd fallen down into the mud, tackled by his friend.

"Hey! Foul!" he said, laughing as he rolled over onto his back.

"Says who?" his friend asked.

"Says me. It's a touch game, remember?"

His friend chuckled. "I'm sorry, was the football distracting you from your new superhero girlfriend?"

"Nah, it's not like that. I think she's cool, that's all."

"*Of course* you think she's cool," Kevin said. "She's an even bigger ham than you are."

"Nothing wrong with being a ham," Tyler replied.

"I'm glad you're so good at being a ham, Ty," Kevin said.

"Yeah," the first one added, right on cue, "because you suck at football."

Tyler clasped both hands to his chest, letting out a strangled noise. "Zounds! I am murdered by thy cruel, cruel words!" Thrashing around, he rolled over on the ground, dying in the most epic of fashions.

Kevin gave him a round of applause. "Bravo! Bravo!"

That only seemed to encourage Tyler, who started to gurgle with his tongue sticking out.

At least until his first friend shoved him down into the mud. It coated half of his face and left him coughing and spitting. "Now you can play the Phantom of the Opera."

Tyler pushed himself up on his hands. "Oh, I see how it is. You were doing me a favor."

"Exactly."

*"Exactly."*

A couple of the boys started howling, as if they were singing opera music. They bent their arms, hiding their noses in their elbows, pretending that they were wearing capes. The game—touch or tackle or otherwise—turned into a complete free-for-all of Phantom versus Phantom.

Tyler was so cute when he laughed.

"That's the spirit!" Captain Superlative said. With a wave, she started to run again, heading away from the game.

Briefly, I considered lingering in the trees, just to watch Tyler. It was what any other girl would do, I was sure.

But with a shake of my head I decided to keep following Captain Superlative.

She continued to fly down the sidewalk. I thought that maybe she was heading home, but at the very edge of downtown, she veered to the left and headed toward the highway. It wasn't a highway, really. But it was the only street in town with more than two lanes—it had a whole four. There were some office buildings peppered in among the apartment complexes. And in the distance, I could see the hospital and the boxy little grocery store.

Was that where Captain Superlative was headed? Was she off to help pack vegetables or recycle cans or escort little old ladies to their cars, carrying their groceries for them? It seemed that way. At least, up until the very last minute.

Captain Superlative went left when she should have gone right, zooming up the cracked walkway that led straight to the front entrance of the hospital. I stopped at the edge of the parking lot, watching as she cut between the parked cars and raced up the concrete ramp, disappearing through the automatic doors that parted for her. My foot hovered in the air, close to stepping down on the blacktop, but I couldn't. I reeled back forcefully, almost losing my balance.

The hospital.

Horrible.

Horrendous.

Hopeless.

No, I thought, clutching the charm on my necklace, I couldn't go there.

On the grassy knoll, across the street from the parking lot, there was a wrought-iron bench. A little gold plaque on the back of the seat announced that it was dedicated in loving memory of Betty Grossman. I didn't know who she was, but I used to imagine that she was enormous, six feet tall and at least three hundred pounds. She had a laugh that rippled through her, shaking the very foundation of Deerwood Park. And she had kind eyes. Like my dad's. I used to draw pictures of them in crayon and colored pencil while lying on my stomach across the bench. I'd spent a lot of time on that bench, I'd had a lot of time to doodle and dream and wonder.

But I hadn't been back in a while.

More than three years.

Not until today. I crossed the street, hurried by the shadow of the hospital on my back. It was the same as ever. I sat on the bench, feeling the coolness of the metal in the January air. Betty's plaque was still there, although the letters had faded a little bit with time. I ran my finger along them, tracing out her name. Apparently, she'd been a loving daughter, sister, wife, and mother.

Like my mother.

*She's gone.*

I'd come out to sit on the bench for the last time when I was nine years old. My mother had just died. Cancer. The memories of that day were blurry, like the shards of shifting glass in a kaleidoscope. Formless. Changing. It made sense, though. At the age of nine, I was just starting to understand things like cancer and death. But not completely. I kept asking, over and over again, how something this unfair could happen. Why? Why her? Why now? And what was going to become of my family? I clung to my dad's arm, terrified that I would lose him too. It made as much sense as anything else at that time. I begged him not to go into the hospital again to get her things. All I could really figure out was that my mother had gone into the hospital and now she wasn't going to come out.

Hospitals were monsters. They gobbled people up. And they were the form of my nightmares. When I was nine. And still sometimes after, although I no longer screamed for my dad to come make it better.

I'd never set foot inside of one. Not since losing my mother. But I could still see the hospital walls, anytime I blinked. Clean and white and impersonal. And with that memory came another, more crystallized and solid.

Third grade. A few days after my mother died. I came back to school to a barrage of drawings, notes, and letters from my classmates. Our teacher, Mr. Fisher, made them put the collection together. He'd even told them what to say. They were scrawled with the same sentence over and over again in marker and crayon and colored pencil:

*I'm glad you're back and I'm really sorry your mother died.*

Every single one.

I tried to get back into the normal routine, doing my times tables and my spelling words. But it was like a bubble of air had been formed around me. My classmates kept their distance. They watched me like some kind of curiosity in a carnival or a strange exhibit in a museum.

And that afternoon, when I sat down on the bench beside April—my best friend in the whole world—to wait for my dad to pick me up, she scooted away from me. She tried to be subtle about it, but third graders (and Aprils) are never subtle. I saw what she did. I saw how terrified she was to let her arm brush against mine. And the way she watched me out of the corners of her eyes, in case I made any sudden movements, in case I tried to come nearer.

When her dad came to pick her up, wearing his crisp blue police uniform, she flung herself at him, full throttle, burying her face in his stomach. He knelt down to ask her what was wrong, but she just started wailing.

That was when I figured it out. They were scared of me. I was different. I was strange.

I was a *freak*.

I blinked myself back into the present, breathing a sigh of relief that that incident had been forgotten.

Mostly.

I was pretty sure April had forgotten we were ever friends, anyway. I hadn't really spoken to her since that day.

And now I imagined Captain Superlative in the hospital,

a splash of color against the sterile white of the corridors, shouting, "Captain Superlative is here to make all troubles disappear!"

If good deeds were her favorite things, then a hospital was definitely the right place for her. I could see her racing through the halls, so busy with tasks that she never stopped for a second, never even noticed the terribleness written across the very walls of the building. She brought patients Jell-O, affectionately telling them that red was the best flavor. She cheered up the nursing staff with cheesy jokes. ("The doctor said to the nurse, 'Did you take that patient's temperature?' The nurse said, 'No, Doctor. Why? Is it missing?' ") It suddenly made sense why she'd so expertly been able to help Kevin in his wheelchair. She was in there, wheeling people from one place to the next on a regular basis, wasn't she?

And she definitely donated blood.

She probably had AB negative, which we'd learned in Science last year was the rarest blood type.

"Have a pint on me," she would say, stretching out her arm, offering up a vein, unafraid of needles or pain.

It was easy to come up with a thousand things she could be doing in there. And exhausting. But what I couldn't figure out was what was behind it all. I knew there had to be something, but... what? All I could say for certain was that she definitely wasn't an alien or a mutant.

I must have been there for hours. I felt stupid just sitting alone on a bench, so I took out my math worksheet and halfheartedly filled in the answers, before turning it over to draw a few tropical starfish like the ones in my dad's waiting room, swimming through a coral reef. I got cold and then numb. And so tired of sitting still. But as the hours ticked by, more and more I found that I couldn't take my eyes off of the automatic doors. Hospitals weren't *really* monsters. I knew that. She had to come out again sometime.

She *had* to.

And she did.

The sun was gone, the slate-gray sky slowly turning to charcoal. It made the red of her cape and the blue of her wig more vivid when she appeared. But what was more shocking was the fact that she wasn't alone. A man and a woman were standing with her, each of them holding one of her hands. The man was wearing a suit, with a tie covered in crisscrossing stripes. He had thin black hair in a ring around his otherwise bald head. The woman was in a gray pencil skirt and high heels, her shiny black hair pulled back behind her head with a big plastic clip.

I don't know why I was so surprised to see them with her. It's not like I really thought that she just rose out of the ocean one day. Even superheroes had to have parents, didn't they?

The three of them made their way through the parking lot. Her dad walked in front, leading the way, while she and her mother followed under a shared umbrella, holding hands. I thought they were heading to a car, but instead they turned onto the sidewalk and started walking back into town. I scooted forward to the edge of the bench, watching them until I was afraid I would lose them. Then I sprang up and started following.

I heard Captain Superlative say something to her mother, but I couldn't understand it. Wolly? Woolly?

Her mother replied. She had a firm but kind voice. The type of voice a strict kindergarten teacher would have. But I couldn't understand her either. I realized that they weren't speaking English. What was it, though? Chinese, maybe?

How would I know?

Her dad looked back over his shoulder and made a remark of some kind. Both of them smiled.

The walk wasn't very long. I noticed that they didn't say much. Captain Superlative and her mother never let go of each other's hand, but there was no small talk, no joking around or teasing. Neither of her parents was asking her about her day. They didn't seem to be playing any games or negotiating what they were going to watch on TV. She wasn't asked to take off her mask, neon wig, and cape. They just walked together until they finally turned up a driveway.

And you know something? Even though I was expecting it to have purple siding and a million flamingos on the front lawn, Captain Superlative's house was about as normal as normal could be. A small, squat redbrick home with a welcome mat on the front step.

And a name on the mailbox.

As Captain Superlative and her parents disappeared through the front door, I spotted it. Written out in gold letters, along the side of the post that held the box: *Li*. My first clue to Captain Superlative's identity, a last name.

Li.

Jackpot!

Joy!

Jubilation!

# 7

**The school library was a big square** room off of the computer lab. One entire wall was made up of windows, looking out into the hallway. The other walls were covered in bookshelves, mostly with reference books, nonfiction, and copies of our textbooks. Along the half of the room closest to the windows were round tables, some with only two chairs, some with up to eight. As I headed inside, I noticed that there was no one sitting at the tables. No surprise, I guess. It was lunch period. But I'd never seen the library look so deserted. There wasn't even a librarian sitting behind the counter. I felt like I was the only living soul in the universe, along with my heartbeat and my breathlessness and my single, solitary purpose.

Rows and rows of bookshelves stretched across the length

of the far end of the room, beyond the tables, like the walls of a neat and orderly garden maze. These were the fiction shelves. But there was another, smaller shelf sitting beside the librarian's desk, with the yearbooks from every class as far back as the school went, from last year all the way back to the black-and-white years. I swiped the yearbook with the red cover, the timber-wolf logo of our school emblazoned across the front. Last year's design. And with a quick glance from side to side, just in case anyone was watching, I dove into the shadows of the bookshelves, hiding from the windows.

Someone named Li. Someone in my grade, whose picture was hidden in the carefully organized rows of photos from last year's sixth graders. I sank down to the ground, resting the yearbook on my thighs, clumsily thumbing through the pages. I couldn't quite figure out if I was nervous or excited. They felt the same. And I couldn't figure out why I would *be* nervous or excited. But I knew that I was close to uncovering the secret of Captain Superlative's identity. And somehow, I was sure, if I could just do that, I could understand why she was so . . . weird.

Li, Li, Li.

The pictures were arranged alphabetically, first by grade, then by last name. And there were only five million Lis among last year's sixth graders. Well. Okay. Maybe six, but it was still a lot. Their unblinking eyes stared up at me from the page. It was easy to eliminate the two boys, but that left four possible girls. I remembered Virginia Li, a girl with a toothy grin and an obsession with all things pink. She'd packed her pink suitcase and moved away last summer, though, when her dad was transferred to another fort. Jennie Li was one of those kids who made it clear that she didn't care about anything except school. She was too busy giving Dagmar a run for her money as top of the class to bother with costumes. Meredith Li was a soccer player, proudly wearing her uniform in her photo. Dagmar and April would have known her in an instant, obviously. Most kids would have. The soccer players were very hard to misplace.

So it was Caitlyn Li who jumped out at me.

She was a petite girl, one I didn't know very well. Vaguely, I seemed to remember that her family had moved to Deerwood Park from China, sometime back in third grade. It was the only thing that had made her remarkable and, after our teacher, Mr. Fisher, made the appropriate introductions, she'd been quickly forgotten. She had a shining curtain of black hair, cut to her shoulders, and delicate, graceful features. Her dark eyes gleamed, like she knew a secret that I didn't know. I slid my index finger over the top of her face, trying to imagine her with a mask and bright blue wig. I could actually see it. Caitlyn Li could be...

Caitlyn! The big *C*! Suddenly it made perfect sense. Maybe the *C* didn't stand for Captain Superlative after all. Maybe it was for Caitlyn?

Beneath each kid's picture was a list of the clubs, teams, and groups they belonged to. Caitlyn Li's list was as long as mine. Which is to say, she didn't seem to belong to any clubs. That was no help, although I guess it explained why no one had identified her yet, as far as I knew.

Underneath the list of clubs, each student had a quote. Caitlyn Li's read, *Have a great summer.*

That explained nothing at all.

But what had I been expecting? "Captain Superlative is here to make all troubles disappear?" That didn't seem likely.

Letting out a slow breath, I started to flip through the back pages of the yearbook, the ones that had candid photos of students just being students. Caitlyn Li popped up once or twice. But if I hadn't been looking for her, I doubt I would have noticed her. In fact, the first few times I stumbled on a picture of her, I realized a minute later it wasn't her at all. I kept hoping to find something, some small bit of information that would crack the code. That would explain why Caitlyn Li just decided, one day, that she was going to be Captain Superlative. But there was nothing. Just like my dad said, she was an ordinary person. An anonymous student. Like me. Another face in the crowd, sitting in the cafeteria, hanging out on the school lawn.

There was nothing superlative about her at all.

My stomach growled. I'd wasted my lunch period looking through a yearbook and come up with nothing but a possible name. Two kinds of hunger warred inside of me. Angry about both of them, I slammed the yearbook shut, setting it on the floor to one side, far away, like I didn't even want to touch it.

"I know you were following me yesterday."

The voice interrupted my sulk so abruptly that I gasped, coughing on my own breath. I looked up, turning my head left and then right. The aisle was deserted. But I knew who it was. I knew her voice.

I knew Captain Superlative was there.

"No, I wasn't," I said. Because that was how you were supposed to respond to things like that.

"Don't lie, Jane." The voice was coming from behind

me. On the other side of the bookshelf. I could just sense her presence somewhere behind my shoulder. "That's not the kind of person you are."

That made me angrier. "How do you know what kind of person I am?" It came out snappish and demanding. "How do you even know my name?" *Especially*, I realized resentfully, when I had been struggling so much to come up with hers.

"It's my job to know these things, citizen," she said.

"No, it's not."

I thought I heard a shrug. "I made it my job. Just like you suddenly made it your job to investigate me."

A flush rose along my cheeks and down the back of my neck. As much as I wanted to deny it, I *had* followed her. And now I was trying to find her in the yearbook. Maybe I'd gone overboard. "I wasn't..." I couldn't come up with an appropriate denial. "I didn't..."

"I don't mind."

Even if it was meant to put me at ease, it didn't. "You don't?" I asked. "Aren't superheroes supposed to guard their secret identities?" It was something my dad would say.

Captain Superlative laughed softly. "Why would I do anything I'm *supposed* to do?"

Good point.

"Besides," she continued, "you're not a very good stalker, you know. I knew what you were doing from the beginning."

"Why didn't you say anything?"

"I was curious. I wanted to see how far you'd go." She paused for a moment, then added, "You didn't follow me into the hospital."

Just when I thought the conversation couldn't get any more uncomfortable, she went and brought my monster into it. "No."

"Why?"

"None of your business," I said hotly, gripping the star-shaped charm on my necklace.

"Are you afraid of hospitals?"

"I *said* it was none of your business." It was a tone my dad wouldn't appreciate, but I didn't care. Maybe I'd crossed some lines, following her, looking for her. But it wasn't the same.

To my surprise, she backed down. "All right, all right."

"I just don't like them, okay?"

"Okay."

Silence followed. I wondered how she'd gotten in without me hearing her. And I wondered if she'd slipped away again, like rainwater leaking in between the cracks of an old roof. But I could somehow still feel her presence behind me. It was a force, an energy. Something I wasn't at all used to feeling. "You're not like the other students here, Jane," she said.

It felt like a compliment, even if it was an insult. "Yes, I am," I said.

"I think you want to be, but you're not. There's something about you that's just a little different. Where does that come from?"

"I'm the same as everyone else," I said, my voice rising above acceptable library levels.

"But—"

"I'm just the same."

I heard her sigh on the other side of the shelf. "If you say so."

"I do."

"Is that why you aren't in any clubs? You don't want to stand out?"

"Can we please stop talking about me?" I paused. "And it's not like you should talk. I don't think you've ever been in a club either."

She laughed. "True." I could sense her hand on the bookshelf. "So what *else* have you dug up?"

The question gave me whiplash. "What?"

"What *else* have you dug up on me? So far."

I looked down at the yearbook. Was she playing some kind of game with me? Was there a joke I didn't understand? I thought about Caitlyn Li's eyes again, gleaming with their secret. It was her, wasn't it? "Your name is Caitlyn Li."

"Well done!" Captain Superlative said, sounding genuinely pleased. "You've found me out!"

"And you weren't in any school clubs."

"That's right! I didn't like standing out back then."

Back then? Well, she certainly did now. I shrugged, up against the shelf, wondering if she could feel my movement on her side of the books. "That's all."

"Not what you were looking for?"

"No." Not even a little bit.

"If you want to know something, you could always ask."

An open invitation. Not an opportunity that came along every day. Which meant that my throat went dry and my mind suddenly felt like clumsy fingers, fumbling and grasping, but unable to grab hold of a thought. "Ask?" I repeated it numbly, overwhelmed by too many possibilities.

"Yes. You could say, 'Captain Superlative, I have a question for you.' And then you could ask your question."

"And if I did? What would happen?"

"I'd answer it."

"Just like that?"

"Just like that."

"Oh." So why couldn't I come up with the question, the thing I really, really wanted to know?

"So-o-o?" she said, drawing out the word into three syllables.

"So..."

"Is there something you'd like to ask me?"

"I—"

*"Captain Superlative,"* she said, prompting.

"Do I have to say 'Captain Superlative'?" The air quotes were implied, since she couldn't see me.

"Yes," she said. "Absolutely."

That was just annoying. All the same, I sighed and tried to pull together the threads of my thoughts. "Captain Superlative..."

What was wrong with me?

"Yes?" she asked encouragingly.

It all coalesced into a single word: *Why?* But that made no sense. It meant too much, it was too big. And I was frustrated that I couldn't collect my thoughts. She'd laugh at me, anyone would. Better to keep those thoughts to myself. Better not to be *that girl*, whatever *that girl* meant at any given time.

"Where'd you get the cape?" I asked dully, picking up the yearbook and pulling myself to my feet.

"That's not what you really want to ask me," she said, sounding like a disappointed teacher.

"Stop acting like you know everything about me!"

*I* didn't even know everything about me. Not yet.

"What's your question, Jane?"

"Nothing! Never mind!"

I stomped along the bookshelves, which felt unnatural considering how hard I usually tried not to make noise. When I came around the side, I expected to see her there, hands on her hips, cape awkwardly draped over her shoulders.

But she wasn't there. There was only an emptiness where her presence had been. The library was deserted again, just me and my frustration.

Fury.

Fixation.

Fascination.

# 8

**There was something unpleasant** clawing around inside of me. It was an untouchable something, which was the worst kind of something imaginable. It was a *feeling*. Yes. A feeling that filled my chest to the brink of suffocating me by the end of the day. A feeling I couldn't exactly name. I guess you could say I felt unhappy. But I didn't know *why* I was unhappy. Something was bothering me, but it wasn't a thing I could change or ignore or even complain about. It just sort of sat on me, pushing the air out of my lungs.

I was drowning in it.

And nobody noticed.

Business as usual in the hallways. Kids were going back and forth, rushing to their lockers, their friends, their after-school clubs. Everything the way it always was, as if nothing was wrong. But something was wrong inside of me and I wanted something to be wrong with everyone else too.

I wouldn't feel so alone that way.

I grabbed books from my locker, shoved them hard into my backpack, and made a beeline for the door. Just outside of the gym, I saw Paige slip out, books piled high in her arms. She actually looked like she was in a good mood. She was smiling—something she rarely did. She looked beautiful.

I wasn't the only one who noticed her good spirits.

Dagmar appeared from around the trophy case, like a supervillain popping out of a cloud of smoke, brimstone swirling around her. Without preamble—or evil laugh—she slammed her hand down on Paige's books, sending them flying across the floor.

It was a more vicious and physical attack than I was used to seeing. It shook me out of my self-pity.

I stopped in my tracks.

"You know you can't win, right?" Dagmar stared at Paige as if she were some kind of maggot or beetle.

"Win?" Paige was bewildered. "What are you talking about?"

"*I'm* going to be top of the class this year. Not Jennie Li. Not Ben Wesson. And *definitely* not you."

Was Paige giving Dagmar a run for her money? News to me. But then, hadn't Captain Superlative said that Paige was a straight-A student? I turned toward the display case, craning my neck so I could watch the reflection of the scene in the glass. At eye level with me, there was an old photograph of a dozen cheerleaders, smiling big at the camera in their matching red uniforms, pom-poms on their hips. Front and center was Dagmar's mother, who looked like a mirror image of Dagmar herself, with her golden curls and her stunning figure. Only the eyes were different. They were warm brown, like a cocker spaniel's. I didn't think they would approve of what they were seeing.

"It's not a contest, Dagmar," Paige said.

"Of course it's a contest. You know it and I know it. Everyone knows it. And I heard you talking to Mr. Collins about going for extra credit."

"That had nothing to do with—"

"*I'm* going to be top of the class. You get it? You're not taking that away from me."

"I wasn't trying to—"

*"Get it?"*

They locked eyes for a moment. I thought Paige was going to fight back. She had a perturbed look to her. Instead, she knelt and started gathering her books. "I don't want to fight with you, Dagmar," she said, her voice barely rising above a whisper.

Dagmar kicked Paige's graphing calculator, sending it skittering across the hall and Paige crawling after it. She watched Paige scrambling, but without her usual air of satisfaction. Apparently, that just wasn't enough. Dagmar tried kicking Paige's social-studies book too. It landed at my feet. That wasn't enough either.

Dagmar folded her arms across her chest, a deep scowl wrinkling up her face, making it look like the craggy slope of a volcano. Her eyes fell on a stack of paper from Paige's pile. "What's this?"

"Dagmar, that's mine!"

She scooped it up just before Paige could snatch it out from under her. "Your paper for Mr. Collins?"

"Let me have that."

"Look at that." Dagmar flipped through it to the last page. In the reflection, I could just see a large, green A-plus, circled in ink. I'd gotten mine back earlier in the day, with an unimpressive B-minus that wasn't circled.

"Give that back!"

She didn't give it back. No. Dagmar Hagen didn't really seem to know the meaning of "subtle" today. She made her intentions quite clear, holding the paper up sideways, her fingertips gripping either end. When she ripped it apart, she moved slowly and deliberately, milking the noise of the tearing papers for everything she could. The students still in the hallway saw and heard what was happening. Most of them ducked their heads, shuffling off as quickly as possible. They created a silent vacuum, an empty space inhabited by only Paige and Dagmar. And the air that was me. I leaned over to pick up Paige's book, some part of me hoping that when I rose again, it would all be over. Dagmar fanned herself with one half of Paige's report. "Get it, Paige?"

"I *did* get it," Paige replied, looking down at the earth beneath her hands. "I got that A-plus. You're just jealous."

"No one's jealous of you, Paige. *You're nothing.* Nobody wants a hobo loser dad," Dagmar said, tossing the ragged paper down at Paige's hunched shoulders.

Paige ignored the remains of her report. She crawled back over to the rest of her things, pulling them carelessly into her arms. Her hands shook. She stood, eyes rising to meet Dagmar's gaze. "I have to get to choir," she said. "Get out of my way."

And then Dagmar crossed a line.

For as long as I could remember, she'd mocked and humiliated Paige, scattered her things, taken cheap shots at her shoes. Insulted her. Posted humiliating pictures online. The same routine, with subtle variations and deviations.

I'd never seen her *hit* Paige before.

It happened so fast. Paige was veering around Dagmar, toward the open hallway. Dagmar pulled back her hand and slapped Paige across the face. The noise was the most incredible part of it. I could hear it echoing through the hall. For half a second, it was the only sound in the world. And then Paige let out a cry of pain and stumbled into the wall, dropping her things again.

"Dagmar!"

"Shut up!"

"Knock it *off*, Dagmar."

But that last part wasn't Paige. It was me. I had spoken. I didn't realize I was opening my mouth until the words were out. My shock was mirrored, first in Paige's eyes and then in Dagmar's, as she turned to look at me over her shoulder, standing beside the picture of her mother, Paige's book trembling in my hands.

I wondered if Dagmar had ever seen my face. We'd been in school together since we were very, very little, but I wasn't sure she'd seen me before. *Really* seen me. There was no question she saw me now, though.

Heard me too.

"What did you say to me?" she asked.

I suppose I could have gotten away clean. I could have said, *Nothing. I didn't say anything.* I could have backed down, hidden my face like Paige. Apologized. Fled. Run away, praying it would all be forgotten. Most kids would have done the same in my situation. In fact, I could only think of one other person in the school who would have done what I ended up doing.

"I *said*, knock it off."

Dagmar's pretty pink lips puckered. Paige was immediately forgotten. Now the golden demon only had eyes for me. "Excuse you," she said. "When did this become your business?"

I didn't have an answer. So I didn't answer. I crossed over to Paige, handing her back her social-studies book. "Here," I said to her.

Paige took it from me. "Thanks."

"I'm *talking* to you," Dagmar said with a snarl.

"Whatever, Dagmar." It was the best I could do. "Just... stop."

"Oh, please."

"Why can't you just leave Paige alone? You're always harassing her. Just... knock it off, already. We're all getting sick of it." I made a broad, sweeping gesture, as if there were a dozen other students in the hallway.

"So you're going to stand up for the loser too?"

I opened my mouth to reply, but someone beat me to the punch.

"Yes. She is."

Once again, she'd crept in unnoticed. Captain Superlative.

Like a true superhero, she'd arrived just in time. I felt her behind my shoulder before I saw her, hands on her hips, chin raised to that magnificent and proud angle. Her eyes glittered with a secret—and when she looked at me, we shared it.

I couldn't remember the last time I'd been a part of a "we" in school.

Dagmar's head whipped from side to side, her eyes looking back and forth between the two of us. "So, there are two *freaks* now."

Somehow it didn't hurt as much as I thought it would. I imagined *freak* feeling like a knife in my chest. But I barely felt it. I almost didn't hear it, actually. "Dagmar," I said, "you are incredibly mean sometimes." Understatement of the century. "Just stop. Stop picking on Paige."

Dagmar's upper lip pulled back from her teeth, and she growled. "Or what?"

"Or we'll stop you," Captain Superlative said simply.

"How?"

My stomach flopped.

*How?* How could we stop a wildfire? I looked over at Captain Superlative. Surely she'd just realized that she'd bitten off more than she could chew—and brought me along for the ride. But the Captain remained calm. "Every time you go near Paige, we'll be there. Maybe you'll think you can sneak an insult in, but you'll be wrong. We'll be watching you, Dagmar. And if you even breathe in her direction the wrong way, if you even think about it..."

An idea started to form in my head. More like an image. "We'll stop you," I said.

"That's right!"

It was brilliant. Simple and elegant. I don't know why I hadn't thought of it before. Probably because I'd never had to try. "We'll be there," I said. "In the hallways, in the auditorium . . ."

"At every soccer game," Captain Superlative added.

"At lunch."

"In gym class."

"Everywhere." I grinned. "And I'll bet you really don't want everyone in the school to see you walking around with two babysitters."

I think Dagmar got the same image in her head that I had. It was the ultimate fall from grace—from popular, from cool—to have the lowest of the low following you around school. Kids who weren't popular—they usually got the message. They stayed away from Dagmar, they lived in fear. But the second that way of things broke down, what would Dagmar be left with?

The two of us.

"Freaks," she said with a sneer. "Only a little nothing would need freaks for protection." She glared at Paige. "*You're nothing.*"

But that was all she could do. That and turn around, stalking away in a huff.

The second she was gone, my insides turned to jelly. I slumped against the trophy case, quivering. It had all happened so fast. I was feeling too much at once to feel anything at all. Except for confused. It was very easy for me to feel very confused about what had just taken place.

Paige, on the other hand, looked delighted. "Thank you, Captain Superlative!" she said, dropping her textbook and throwing her arms around Captain Superlative's shoulders. They hugged. Just like any two ordinary girls on an ordinary day in an ordinary school. With her back to me, with her mask partly hidden by Paige's head, Captain Superlative could have been anyone.

Well. Anyone in a bright blue wig.

When they pulled apart, Captain Superlative put a hand on Paige's shoulder. "Think nothing of it, citizen."

And then they were both looking at me.

"You too, Jane," Paige said, a bit shy. "I never thought that..."

The way she trailed off made me uncomfortable. "What?"

"Nothing." Paige shook her head. "Just, thank you."

"You're welcome?"

By this point, Captain Superlative had collected all of Paige's books. She handed them off and Paige smiled prettily at me, before turning around and hurrying away for choir practice.

There was something different in the way she walked. I couldn't put my finger on it at first. Just the expression on her face—and the fact that I could see her face at all.

I felt Captain Superlative's eyes on me and I turned to look at her. She was grinning, the mask raised slightly on her forehead. "What?" I asked, squirming from one foot to the other.

"That was an incredible thing you did, Jane."

I shrugged. "Dagmar crossed a line."

"A line?" the Captain asked.

"She shouldn't have hit Paige. It was wrong."

"What she's been doing to Paige has *always* been wrong."

"Yeah, but—"

"Is there a difference between pain you can see and pain you can't see?"

"I..."

She shook her head. "Don't worry. We'll work on it. The point is that *you* stood up to her. Finally."

"Finally?"

"I've been waiting for this day." She clapped her hands together in front of her chest. "Oh, Jane. I was so hoping it would be you. I was so sure it would be when you followed me!"

"What? Me?" It felt like a hand was closing over my throat, cutting off my air. "What are you talking about?"

"You're the one I've been waiting for." She walked over to me, planting a firm hand on my shoulder before I could slip away. "Jane." She said the name with a hushed reverence. "You are going to be my sidekick."

"What?!"

"Every good superhero needs one."

I pulled away from her, sliding along the wall and circling around so I could feel the open hallway at my back. "I am not a sidekick!" I said. My voice was rising into a whine.

"Not yet! But today, without even realizing it, you took your first steps into sidekick-dom. Oh, Jane, I'm so happy!"

I thought I was free and clear, but she was surprisingly fast. Captain Superlative threw her arms around me, pulling me into a tight embrace against her chest. For someone so little, she had a powerful hold. And she smelled like toasted almonds. It reminded me of an old bottle of my mother's perfume that my dad kept on the nightstand in his room. Sweet, but not cloying. Sort of light. Warm.

"No," I said, weakened by the memory, pulling out of her arms. "No. I'm not . . . I don't . . ."

If she heard my protestations, she ignored them. "I can't wait to start your training!"

"No!" I put more force into my voice as the scent faded. "You don't get it. I'm not like you!"

Captain Superlative grinned. "That's where you're wrong, Jane."

"What?" I gripped my necklace.

"You are! You *are* like me! You're exactly like me! We start your training tonight!"

"No!" I was practically screaming, but on a Friday afternoon, there were very few people left in the school to hear. And evidently, no one seemed to care. "No, no, no! Absolutely not!"

"You think you're afraid. But trust me, Jane, you're now the second-bravest person in the school. And I'll bet, with just a little bit of time and practice, you'll be just as brave as me! Superlative brave!" She seemed so completely, bewilderingly proud as she looked at me. But in a flash, she turned around, raising her arms over her head again, prepared to take flight. "Captain Superlative is here to make all troubles disappear!" she shouted.

And off she zoomed.

I didn't know which was worse: the flood or the fire. But either way, I was in a lot of trouble.

# 9

**I told the story to my dad that night as** we folded the bedsheets, still warm from the dryer. Every excruciating detail, although I left out the part where Dagmar slapped Paige. I knew my dad, and I knew that if he heard anything like that, he'd be on the phone with the school in the blink of an eye. After we'd helped save Paige, I didn't want to let Paige be destroyed. If Dagmar got called out, she'd lose favor with the teachers. And then she'd be even more convinced that Paige was trying to beat her for top of the class or something. Paige would never hear the end of it.

And she'd already suffered plenty.

"And then what happened?" Dad asked, drinking in every single word of the story with a hushed sense of awe.

"And then we said we'd follow Dagmar around the school to make sure she never had the chance to pick on Paige,"

I said. "I don't think she liked the idea of having a superhero follow her like some kind of puppy."

"Of course not." Dad chuckled. "What would people think?"

I gave him a thin smile. At least he seemed to think the whole thing was funny. "Exactly."

"Bravo, Janey," he said. "A-plus." And he touched his ear.

"Admiration?"

"Absolutely."

"Astonishment?"

"Adoration." I wrinkled my nose, not entirely convinced it was a real word. My dad laughed again. "I'm so proud of you, Janey."

"Oh, stop it."

"No, really, I am."

I picked up a rumpled sheet, holding a corner to him. He took it and we spread out across the living room, smoothing it like the surface of a frozen lake. "You're making a big deal out of nothing."

"Am I?"

"Yes," I said, folding my end as he folded his. "You *and* Captain Superlative both are."

"Well, I think it was a fantastic thing you did. Standing up for Paige like that. You've been telling me for years how Dagmar's been picking on her. I always hoped that one day, you'd—"

"I wish everyone would just forget about it." I tried to say it bashfully, laughingly. Like it was no big deal. Just a little joke. A funny little story that would fade away soon enough.

But it came out shrill. Maybe even somewhat panicked. The truth was that I was a little scared.

I was *a lot* scared.

My visions of Dagmar mistreating Paige had begun to change over the last few hours. I wasn't seeing Paige's face in them anymore. I was seeing my own. Now Dagmar was kicking *my* towel into the pool during summer camp. She was making fun of *my* jeans. She was throwing *my* training bra into the boys' locker room. It had all happened so fast. Too fast. Only now was I really, truly allowing myself to realize what I'd done.

And regret it.

My dad glanced up at me under his bushy eyebrows. It was unusual for him to let me get away with interrupting without at least an arched brow. But for once, he didn't seem up to scolding me. "I don't think Paige will," he finally said, softer and milder than usual.

"Yeah."

"Why's it bothering you so much?"

"It's not *bothering* me," I said. Maybe a little too quickly.

"Janey."

I sighed. If I couldn't talk about this with my dad, who could I talk about it with? No one, really. Maybe Selina, if she wasn't hiding under a dresser somewhere. But really, she wasn't great at giving advice, being a cat and all. "I'm just pretty sure Dagmar's close to exploding over the whole thing," I said. "That's all."

"I see," he said, walking over to me to take my corners of the sheet. "And you're afraid of what she'll do?"

"Yeah. A little."

My dad finished folding the sheet by himself, adding it to the growing pile of linen on the coffee table. "Seems like you've lost some of that anonymity you loved so much, Janey."

"Maybe."

"But maybe you traded it in for something even better," he said. "Something . . . superlative."

Oh, that word.

I sat down on the corner of the coffee table, picking up one of the blue pillowcases and laying it out across my lap. I always folded them the same way. Left edge pulled over, then the right edge. Then fold it down the middle and set it on the pile, open ends all lined up and facing the same way. For some reason, though, my hands forgot the routine. They hovered above the sheet, until my dad reached over, pulling up on the left edge for me. I don't know why, but for some reason, I felt like I was going to cry.

For forgetting how to fold laundry?

What was *wrong* with me?

Dad sat down on the table next to me, wrapping his arm around my waist and squeezing me gently against his side. "Tell me something, though," he said. "What did you mean when you said Captain Superlative was making too much of a big deal out of nothing?"

"Oh."

"What?"

"It's *so* ridiculous," I said, swallowing hard.

"Janey?"

"She says . . . she says she wants to make me her sidekick."

"Her sidekick?" Both bushy eyebrows went up.

"Yeah."

He let out a loud belly laugh, so abrupt and sudden that it shook the framed wedding photograph and my inked baby footprints on the bookshelf. "Well, that's wonderful!"

I rolled my eyes. "I knew you'd say something like that."

"It's perfect."

I looked up at him out of the corners of my eyes. "Shouldn't you be concerned for my safety or something, like a *normal* parent?"

"Nonsense. This is perfect. I always dreamed you'd grow up to be someone important. Either a superhero or vice president."

"Stop it," I said, trying not to laugh.

"I'm serious."

"She says she's going to start training me." I could only shake my head. "I wonder what that would involve."

"Oh, all the important things a superhero's sidekick needs to know how to do, no doubt."

"Like what?"

"Like . . . rescuing intrepid reporters."

"What?"

He stood up, grabbing a corner of the pillowcase and whirling around, letting it unfold and flutter behind him. He tied it around his shoulders like a cape. Before I could even register surprise, he'd scooped me up in a fireman's hold, his arm under my knees, and was running in tight circles around the coffee table, one fist punching into the air. Out of the side of his mouth, he made a whooshing noise. "Up we go!"

I shrieked, holding on for dear life, my fingers digging into the back of his shirt. "Dad!"

"Don't worry, Ms. Silverman. You're safe with me!"

"What are you doing?!"

"Flying!"

"Dad."

"Up into the stratosphere!"

"Dad!"

"Look! I can see our house from up here!"

"Dad!"

"What?"

"She doesn't know how to fly!"

He stopped in his tracks, his heart racing in his chest against my arm. "Oh. Not a flying hero? Drat."

"Put me down!"

He set me down on my feet, on top of the coffee table. "There are other skills to hone too, of course."

I couldn't help myself. "What else?"

"Learning to knock the metal tab off of a can of pop with a bow and arrow, without spilling a drop! Just like in the movies."

"What?!"

"You know." He flexed his muscles before miming the graceful dance of pulling back the string of a bow. Out of the side of his mouth, he started humming a song I didn't know, taking aim. And then he let loose a few make-believe arrows. "Zing! Zing! Kaboom! That one was an exploding arrow!"

"Dad!"

"Arrows against the school code of conduct? Never mind! There's always sword training!" From his hip, he drew an imaginary sword, wielding it in a flowing arc over his head. "Right for might!"

"Are you kidding me?"

"What? This is the money shot!" He let out a few hisses. "Listen to the screaming of the paparazzi! They're going wild! They're climbing over each other, trying to get my picture!"

"Stop it!"

"C'mon, Janey." He held out his invisible sword, like he expected me to take it. "Join in. You're going to need this training."

"Dad!"

"Listen to them! They're calling out your name!" He cupped his hands around his mouth. "'Janey! Janey! Janey!'"

I didn't want anyone calling out my name. "Dad, seriously, stop." My feet sucked against the glass as I sat back down on the edge of the coffee table. "I'm not going into training. I already told her that."

He finally dropped his arms and plopped down next to me again. The pillowcase fell off of his back. "Why not, Janey?"

Because I didn't want to. But I knew an answer like that wouldn't land well. "She'll probably just forget about it," I said instead, reaching behind him to grab the pillowcase. I started to refold it. "She's got to be working on some big new stunt to pull next week. She's got to top herself. Can't be easy."

"Do you think so?" he asked, draping his arm over my shoulders.

"Yeah."

"Well. Maybe." But then he leaned in close, resting his head against mine. "Or that might be wishful thinking, my dear."

"Maybe."

A sharp buzz from the intercom on the wall shot through our talk. Simultaneously, my dad and I put our fingers to our noses. "Not it!" I said, a second before he could.

"Rats!" he said, snapping his fingers. "Defeated!"

"You snooze, you lose."

Dad let out an exaggerated groan, stood up, and put both hands on the small of his back to stretch. "Oh well. Serves me right for tangling with a genuine superhero. In training."

"Dad!"

"I kid. I kid! Like a goat, I kid." He let out a noise that I assumed he thought sounded vaguely like a goat. And then, as was expected of the loser, he trudged to the entryway to see who had buzzed.

It was most likely Chad Goldstein, I thought. The kid who lived across the hallway and always forgot his keys. Dad was nice to him, let him back in the building when his parents were out for the night. Chad was, I guess, almost like a friend. We always smiled at each other in the stairwell, anyway. The perfect kind of friend. The kind that couldn't betray me or turn his back on me.

I was smiling again, the unpleasant feelings that had been eating at me throughout the day finally fading away as I reached out to fold another pillowcase, the same way I always folded pillowcases.

I should have known.

I *really* should have known. I'd been around Captain

Superlative enough. I knew what she was. A riptide. Anyone and anything that came into her path immediately got pulled in. There was no escaping it.

"Oh, Ja-aney!" my dad called from the little narrow entryway in a singsongy voice.

"What?" I called back.

"You have a visitor."

A visitor? Me? No one ever came over to visit me. Not unless it was for some group assignment or something. I spent five seconds trying to figure it out. It was in the sixth second that she appeared in the door to the living room, my dad standing behind her, grinning.

"The Captain would like to see you."

# 10

**"Hello!" she said, hands on her hips,** chin raised, smiling wildly at me from behind her mask.

Captain Superlative. In my home. My brain couldn't exactly reconcile it. Seeing anyone here—other than me and Dad—was weird enough. But this? Calling her a fish out of water wouldn't do. It was more like another story had just crashed into my book and the style of illustration was completely different. It was a surrealist drawing in the middle of my still life. She clashed with everything, the bright neon pink of her winter coat blinding against the calm and neutral colors of our walls, the energy she brought with her too powerful for our quiet lives.

Uncomfortable silence followed, until my dad cleared his throat. "Say hello to your guest, Janey." It was the same tone of voice he'd used when I was six and had to be goaded into giving Aunt Stephanie a kiss on the cheek.

"Hello," I said.

"We have important work to do," Captain Superlative said. "Your sidekick training needs to begin."

I looked over at my dad, desperate to get him to share in the joke and show that he understood my plight. Instead, his grin just got broader, pleased as could be. "I'll leave you to it," he said.

I started talking immediately, before I even knew what it was I wanted to say. "I really don't think tonight is a good night." Words came tumbling out. "I mean, I have a lot of math homework. And I need to finish reading chapter nine of *Number the Stars*. And there's a science lab due next week. And I have that big social-studies test coming up on Monday. And I really should be studying for—"

"I made you a study guide!" Captain Superlative said, pulling a folded-up packet of papers out of her coat pocket.

"She made you a study guide," my dad said, beaming at me.

Captain Superlative thrust it at me, leaving me no choice but to take it. It was the same as the one April had shown Dagmar, with the red staple in the corner. The question about ostracism was right up at the top. "Oh," I said, staring at it.

"It's a Friday night," my dad said. "Have some fun for once in your life. Get out of your routine. You're in a rut, Janey."

"Oh, it'll be super-fun!" Captain Superlative said.

"I think I'll just go put the laundry away," my dad said, walking over to pick up the pile beside me on the table.

Quickly, I dropped the study guide and reached out to grab one of the pillowcases. "You know it's my turn to change the beds."

"I think I can handle it tonight." My dad put his hand over mine, prying my grip loose.

Captain Superlative saluted my dad. "Thank you, citizen."

He saluted right back. "You're most welcome, Captain." He dropped the neatly folded sheets in the laundry basket, hefting it up on his hip. As he started to go, he paused and looked back over his shoulder at her. "Tell me something."

"Yes?"

"Do superheroes like brownies?"

She grinned. "We do!"

"Well, then. How about I go whip up a batch of my triple-fudge-chunk brownies?" My favorites. The ones that Dad only made for special occasions—birthdays and holidays and celebrations.

Tonight wasn't a special occasion. There was nothing to celebrate.

"That would be wonderful!" Captain Superlative said. She didn't understand. These were *special* brownies. "Thank you, Dr. Silverman!"

"Of course," my dad said. "Anything to do my part for the cause. And please, call me Robert. I only make my patients and Janey call me Dr. Silverman."

"Your patients are dogs and cats, Dad," I said.

Captain Superlative, however, found the joke hilarious. "Really?" she asked, laughing.

"Really," he said.

"All right." She looked at me. "And should I call you Janey?" she asked me.

"That's her name," Dad said.

"Then that's what I'll call you," she said to me. Back to my dad. "Thanks, *Robert*."

"I'll be in the kitchen," he said.

And with that, my dad sauntered out of the room, whistling the same old song he'd been humming before.

The Captain and I were alone.

# 11

**"We have so much work to do!"** Captain Superlative was already wiggling out of her downy coat, revealing the cape, swimsuit, and tights underneath.

"I think you have the wrong idea about me," I said. It came out more like a plea than anything else.

"Nonsense!" She dumped her backpack on the floor and knelt beside it, yanking open the zipper. A pile of comic books came slipping out, the glossy covers sliding all over the carpet. I recognized some of the titles from my dad's collection: *Hawkgirl* and *Batman* and *Wonder Woman*.

"Captain Sup . . ." I stopped. If I didn't want to be a part of this game, why was I even playing it? "Caitlyn."

"Captain Superlative!"

"Whatever. I'm not really interested in being a superhero. I don't think I'm in a 'superhero' kind of place."

She laughed. "That's why you're only a sidekick." She picked up one of her comics, which had a statuesque woman and a younger girl dressed in similar costumes on the cover. She thrust it into my hands and jabbed at the girl, presumably the sidekick, with one finger. "You'll have to work your way up to hero, Janey."

Hearing someone other than my dad say "Janey" struck me for a second. It sent a small shiver up my spine. "It's just not my thing," I said, trying to ignore the feeling.

I attempted to shove the comic book back into her hands, but she pushed it away. "Okay. What *is* your thing?" she asked.

The question gave me pause. My thing? My thing? I didn't really have a thing. Dagmar was a soccer player and Tyler was a drama kid and Captain Superlative ran around like a cartoon character, and, apparently, Paige wrote beautiful songs. Me? I just kind of drifted. I was just the air.

But that wasn't the point!

I shook my head fiercely, angry at her for getting me sidetracked and angry at myself for letting her do it. "I don't want to—"

"We'll begin with the easy stuff. Let's talk about door opening."

It was bad enough she was here and wasn't listening to me. But now she was just patronizing me. I felt my skin crawl. "I *know* how to open doors," I said, my teeth grinding together.

"Brilliant! You're already ahead of the curve."

"They're *just* doors."

"Not just doors!" She grabbed one comic book after another, opening to pages of monsters and demons and supervillains in brightly colored spandex, with maniacal grins and elaborate devices and thought bubbles with jagged, sharp edges. "Monsters! Giant beasts! Great obstacles that must be defeated in the most superheroical of fashions! Biff! Pow! Whack!"

She threw a few air punches.

I could feel the frustration bubbling inside of me. It was ready to explode, to come out like a geyser. But when it did, I surprised myself. And I surprised her. Because the eruption took the form of a question:

"Why do you do it?"

It was the first time I'd ever seen Captain Superlative caught off guard. Even with her mask on, she seemed startled by the question, looking up from the colorful pages. "What?"

"Why do you do these things? Why are you running around in a cape and tights? It isn't normal."

For a second, she stared at me. Silence hung thickly between us. Then she started to wander around the room, examining the bookcase with my baby footprints and the starry landscape I'd painted years ago. Her gaze fell on the picture of my parents, and for some reason, I was afraid that she would touch it. But Captain Superlative was respectful. It was almost like she was bowing her head to them. I was ready to stomp my foot and demand an answer. "That's a question that's been bothering you for a while, hasn't it?" she finally said, her back to me.

I gripped my necklace. "Yeah."

"I thought so." Her gaze fell on the comic book my dad had shown me a few days ago, with the star-covered hero, resting up on the shelf. "Sweet pants! Is this a first edition?"

She reached out like she was going to grab it, but then pulled back her hand, fingers twitching with desire.

"Yeah, I guess," I said, working my thumb over the blue bead in the charm. I should have asked in the library, I thought. I should have worked up the nerve then. Maybe we wouldn't be having this conversation now. Maybe we wouldn't be having this conversation *here*. "Why?" I asked again. "Why are you always helping people?"

"I'll bet you can figure it out."

I hated it when people did that, when they answered a question by challenging me to answer it myself. She reminded me of a teacher, nudging me to solve a word problem. And the most annoying part of it was that I found myself going along with it and thinking out loud, like I was really trying to piece together the puzzle. "People can open their own doors," I said, staring at the big *C* on her cape.

"Yes, I know."

"And find their own way through the school."

"Sure, eventually."

"So why are you doing these things?"

"Well, they are nice things to do, for one thing," she said. "And superheroes are almost always nice."

"Yeah. But these things are so . . ."

"Small?"

"Yeah. It's not really what superheroes do." There weren't comic books of guys in tights helping little old ladies cross a street. Or opening a door for strangers. Not that I knew of any cartoony time bombs in Deerwood Park that needed deactivating in the nick of time. Although I was sure she'd be there to cut the red wire, or whatever.

Captain Superlative laughed, turning around to face me again. She trotted over to the recliner, sitting on the very edge of the seat, leaning in so that our faces were only inches apart. "Why would you think there's a difference between the big things and the small things?"

I pulled away, uncomfortable with the closeness, with the intimacy of the question. Looking to one side, I saw Selina poke her little black face through the doorway, letting out a gentle, inquisitive mew. "Because there *is* a difference. That's why they're called 'big' and 'small' in the first place. Not everything is a . . . a . . ."—my hand fluttered in her direction—"superlative!"

Supreme.

Sensational.

Special.

To her credit, she didn't press forward. She let me have my space, but not my opinion. "It's all the same." She flopped back against the soft, puffy seat of the recliner, her legs straightening out and dangling above the ground, the hair of her wig fanning out around her face like a blue halo. "Good is good. And good is a habit. You have to get into it. And sometimes, the best way to do that is with the little stuff. Holding a door open for someone who can't. Or pointing the way to the cafeteria to a new kid who's lost on the first day."

At first, I was ready to call that kindergarten logic. But then, so was learning the letters of the alphabet before you learned how to spell words. "I guess that sort of makes sense."

"And once you get into the habit, then you can start on the bigger, better, bestest things," Captain Superlative continued. "Like standing up to Dagmar Hagen when she's picking on someone." She paused for a second, curling her hand up into a fist and coughing into it. "You're a prodigy, Janey." She sounded proud, if not a little wheezy. "You jumped right into the deep end. Without even knowing it." She cleared her throat. "I'll bet you get that from your father. He seems like a super-duper, first-rate sort of guy."

The corners of my lips twitched, just slightly. She'd only been in his presence five minutes, at most. But she was sharp. "Yeah. He's great. I mean, ever since my mother died, he's always been there."

"I knew it, I knew it!" She sat up straight again on the edge of the seat. "'Always been there.' That's what heroes do! It must run in the family!"

The more I listened to her, the more I wanted to like her. It wasn't so much the things she said as the way she said them. I'd never met anyone so sure, so confident. Like she didn't even know how to hesitate. But she was wrong to be confident about me. I knew it. "Look." I genuinely felt sorry to disappoint her. "What I did with Dagmar was a mistake."

"A mistake?"

"I don't know what her problem with Paige was—"

"No one knows what her problem with Paige *is*," Captain Superlative said. "Although I'll bet her problem with Paige isn't really with Paige at all."

I had no idea what that meant. "It wasn't my place to interfere."

Her frown pulled down the edges of her mask. Selina jumped up onto the arm of the recliner beside Captain Superlative, rubbing the top of her head against her arm. "I don't understand," she said, absently stroking the velvety fur between Selina's ears.

"I had no right to tell Dagmar how to behave." I gripped the edges of the comic book in my hands, my fingers turning white. "I should have minded my own business."

Same as everyone else.

Captain Superlative set her elbow on the arm of the chair, resting her chin on her knuckles. Selina shoved her head under Captain Superlative's arm, rubbing up against her belly and purring. I don't think I'd ever seen her quite so desperate to get someone's attention. She usually ran away when Dad had visitors. We wouldn't see her again for hours, until she crept out of the shadows for something to eat.

"But what would have happened to Paige?" Captain Superlative asked, giving Selina the affection she demanded.

"I..."

What would have happened to Paige? Vignettes appeared in my mind each time I blinked. I saw Paige getting shoved headfirst into a locker. I saw Paige getting kicked with the squeaky plastic of Dagmar's Blue Shoes. Paige curled up in tears on the floor. Or huddling in a corner of the bathroom, hugging her books to her chest, her beauty hidden by welts or bruises or swollen eyes, silently praying for the earth to open up and swallow her.

Captain Superlative seemed to be reading my mind. A dark look crossed the part of her face that I could see. It felt like despair. "That's the problem with the world. Everyone seems to think that doing a good deed is someone else's job. It doesn't matter so much for the little things, maybe. No one's life is going to change if someone else opens the door for them. But when you start to get into the bigger things . . . well. If everyone said it wasn't their place to stand up to Dagmar, then nobody would stand up to her at all. And people like Paige?" She shook her head solemnly. "They wouldn't have a chance."

I felt like something was squeezing the air out of my chest, my throat. It wasn't an accusation, I knew that. But it still was, in a way. "She could tell a teacher," I said softly, practically croaking. Somehow, putting the responsibility back on Paige felt like an escape, a way to avoid looking at what I'd done. Or rather, what I mostly *hadn't* done up until today.

"But she doesn't."

"It's a teacher's *job* to stop these things from happening," I said.

"Yes," she said, "but the problem is, Dagmar is clever."

"Clever?"

"If a teacher sees her picking on Paige in a classroom, *of course* that teacher is going to do something. Like you said, that's part of the job. But Dagmar chooses her opportunities carefully."

I knew. Somehow I'd always known. "The hallways."

"The most dangerous part of the school."

"There's no teacher in charge there."

"Exactly. Being in the hallways is like being in a black hole or the Bermuda Triangle. And not only does Dagmar choose the opportunities carefully, but she chooses her victims carefully too. Paige, for example, never says anything to anyone. And since she doesn't, and nobody else does, all those horrible things Dagmar does just get blown away in the wind."

Lost in the air. I was the air. I stood up, uncomfortable in my own skin again. I'd seen Dagmar at it more times than I could count. I'd taken it for granted as much as breathing. It was a part of life, a fact. A certainty.

Again, Captain Superlative gave me my space, watching me from her perch on the recliner, Selina puddled in her lap. "It doesn't help that all the teachers love Dagmar," she added. "It makes it feel almost impossible to tell the truth about her." Her voice grew subdued, quiet. Normal, really. And sad. "There's nothing worse in the world than realizing that no one can help you."

I wasn't sure she was talking to me. She'd gone somewhere else, somewhere inside, I think. But in the next minute, she was back again, the confidence bolstering her tone once more. "Well. Not anymore. The world needs more people like us, Janey. People who are willing to get into the habit of doing good things instead of just breezing by."

I stopped by the bookcase, looking at my mother in her wedding dress. "I never really thought about it before."

"I know. Most people don't."

"But you do?" I asked, turning to her.

She coughed again, before nodding. "Yes."

"Why?" The whys were becoming easier, even if hearing the answers wasn't easy at all.

But Captain Superlative shrugged. "I just do. It's who I am." With that, she picked up Selina and bounced up from the chair, making her way over to me. She was probably about three inches shorter than me, but she felt enormous. Or maybe I was just feeling very, very small at the moment. "What do you say, Janey? Do you want to change the world?"

I frowned, biting down on my lower lip. "I'm not sure that it's me."

"And you're not sure that it's *not* you either!" she said. "You don't know until you try. *Try* something, Janey! Try *something*!"

I thought about my own picture in the yearbook. No clubs or activities listed. I thought about how surprising it was to have someone come to visit me. And I thought about the look on Paige's face today when someone had come to her rescue in the hallway. When *we'd* saved her. "It did feel kind of good, making Dagmar stop."

"Life is too short to be anything less than superlative. C'mon, Janey. Give it a shot."

"I..."

"Your kitty wants you to join me. Listen to her." She held up Selina, bouncing her a little bit. "Join the quest!" she said, speaking in a ridiculous kitty-cat voice. "I want you to hang out with Captain Superlative."

Selina tolerated it surprisingly well.

"Say yes." She returned to her normal voice. "Come on. Say yes. Be superlative!"

Air didn't say yes or no. Air just existed. But maybe it was time for me to try something different. I found myself looking down at the comic book in my hands. The mighty lady and her loyal and eager sidekick were so confident, so carefree. So happy. They were running, the wind blowing their hair back, powerful muscles carrying them who-knew-where, on toward adventure. Forward. Maybe, just maybe, I could be something like that, *feel* something like that.

"Yes."

"Wonderful!"

I held up a hand. "But," I said sharply, "I'm not wearing a costume."

Captain Superlative shook her head, smiling. "You don't have to!"

"And I'm not picking a new name."

"But that's half of the fun."

"I like my name."

"All right." She tucked Selina into the crook of her arm and held out a hand to me. "Sidekick?"

I took it. "Deal."

We shook hands.

Our conspiring began over brownies, comic books, and study guides for the social-studies test. We must have been whispering and giggling almost to midnight. When Captain Superlative left, she gave me another hug and told me how proud of me she was. My cheeks flushed with heat, with warmth. In all of the excitement of beginning something new, though, I forgot that I'd never really gotten an answer to my question. I didn't know why she'd suddenly decided to just be a superhero. It didn't matter.

I chose Captain Superlative. I chose the flood.

And that's how it might have ended. But instead, it was just the beginning.

Birth.

Becoming.

Being.

# 12

"Hi, Janey!" Captain Superlative called loudly from the other side of the front atrium. It was Monday morning and the sunlight was reflecting off the snow, filling the entry hall with blindingly white light. She was standing at the entrance to the seventh-grade hall, shining bright silver, handing out packets of paper to the kids as they passed her, disrupting and stirring the motes of dust.

A few kids glanced back and forth between the two of us, but no one said anything. I didn't know what to expect when I walked into school and everyone saw me with her. And on purpose. When no one responded, I realized that I still had a choice. Oh, sure, I'd signed on to this crusade under the velvety cover of a dark Friday night, but in the clear light of day, there was an opportunity before me to back out. It seemed like the sort of thing Jane would have done. But if my father was right, if I really was *Janey!* and some kind of hero-in-waiting, then I was going to move forward.

The decision was made.

I walked over to Captain Superlative's side and she handed me a stack of papers—study guides for the big social-studies test with gleaming red staples. The two of us had gone over and over the vocab words on Friday. I'd never spent so much time studying for a test in my life, never felt so prepared to walk into Ms. Hinton's classroom. I gave Captain Superlative a skeptical look, though. "Isn't it a little late for these? The test is today."

"It's never too late!" she said. "And I felt bad. I only made them for the kids in my class, but everyone could use them."

Shrugging, I took my stack and started to hand out the guides. For a few minutes, it was surprisingly uneventful, anticlimactic. Even a little boring.

Then I heard it.

Dagmar's voice seared through the morning buzz. "Wait. There are *two* of them now?"

Dagmar approached us from the main entrance, with April trailing behind her. They wore matching peacoats and matching Blue Shoes. Kids stepped out of the way, lingering on the sidelines to see what was going to happen. Dagmar looked particularly regal. Her curly hair was pulled into a tight braid that crossed over the top of her head, a bit like a crown. The aristocratic sneer on her face was exaggerated by the bright red of her lipstick.

Naturally, Captain Superlative was unafraid. "Good morning, Dagmar," she said brightly, offering her one of the study guides.

Dagmar snatched the guide out of her hand and crumpled it up, all in one blazing movement. She tossed the guide to the floor, crushing it under the heel of her Blue Shoe. Kids gasped and shifted in the crowd, hoping to slip away unnoticed. Even April, standing behind Dagmar's shoulder, looked surprised.

Panic flooded into my chest. I turned to Captain Superlative. What happened now? The queen had spoken.

Calm as ever, Captain Superlative turned to April and offered her a guide from the pile. April reached to take it, but Dagmar got in the way. "No one wants your study guides." Her gaze passed back and forth between us, no interest in April's feelings on the matter.

"That's not true," Captain Superlative said. "Really, it's just that *you* don't want our help. And that's okay. You're a straight-A student. You'll probably ace the test. But if anyone else wants a guide, they're more than welcome to have one."

I'm not sure who was more thrown by Captain Superlative's placid reply—me or April or Dagmar. Dagmar sputtered, her cheeks turning pink. *"No one,"* she repeated, "wants your study guides."

"You don't speak for everyone, Dagmar." I said it without thinking. *Again*. Just like the Friday before with Paige. This time, I had no regrets. And I had an audience.

Ripples of surprise passed through the other seventh graders. "You really don't, Dagmar," someone said.

"Yeah," several others agreed.

Suddenly there was a chorus of murmuring. Even April nodded her head. Just slightly. Kids were siding with *us* over Dagmar Hagen.

*Dagmar Hagen.*

"I'll take a study guide," said a thin voice. Paige walked over to the hallway entrance, her books folded into the crook of her arm. Her cornrows were gathered in a green ribbon at the base of her neck. I had a feeling she didn't need a study guide, but she—of all people—didn't have anything to lose standing up to Dagmar. Captain Superlative handed her a guide, and with a smile thrown in my direction, Paige headed off to her first class.

The dam broke. Our classmates started lining up on either side of the entrance, getting louder and louder as they asked us to pass them guides.

"Ms. Hinton always puts trick questions on her tests."

"I totally forgot to study."

"Wait, that test is *today*?"

Dagmar stood between the two lines, her lips slightly parted as her kingdom began to crash around her. April caught my eye, giving me a slight smile. It was the same smile she used to give me when my father told a particularly bad joke. As if everything that happened in third grade and after hadn't happened at all. As if we were suddenly friends again.

The warning bell rang. The hallway exploded into a chaotic mess. We ran out of guides as our classmates snatched the last few and raced off to homeroom. Dagmar remained still, statuelike. Her hands gripped her hips. Her eyes fixed on us. "You shouldn't have done that."

"Aw, calm down, Dagmar. It's not a big deal." Tyler Jeffries walked our way, his backpack casually draped over one shoulder. Dagmar immediately transformed, putting on the same sugary-sweet smile she used to charm the teachers.

Tyler didn't give her a second glance.

He was walking toward . . . me. Directly toward *me.* I thought my eyes might bulge out of my head. "You have any study guides left? Ms. Hinton's tests are absolute murder."

He was talking. To *me.*

A strangled squeak threatened to bubble up out of my throat. Dazed and numb, I reached into my own bag. "Here," I said. "You can have mine."

He smiled. "Thanks. But I don't want to take your—"

"No, I'm good," I said, practically shoving it in his hands. "I think I can take the test in my sleep at this point."

"We studied all weekend," Captain Superlative said.

Tyler chuckled. "You're smarter than I am," he said. "The only time I even *thought* about the Greeks this weekend was when I got chicken gyros at the Hawthorne food court."

I laughed. "The only time?"

"Remind me, who's the god of war again? Is it Tzatziki?"

"Pretty sure that's a sauce."

He snapped his fingers. "Dang, I really should have studied."

"I think you'll do all right."

"Guess we'll find out." He slipped the study guide into his bag and started to walk away. He looked back, over his shoulder. "Moussaka's the god of the sea, right?"

"Poseidon!"

His eyes lingered for a second longer before he turned, nodding to Captain Superlative. Then he was gone, pumping his fist in the air in triumph.

I might have drifted off into a wonderful fog, except

Dagmar was still posed in front of us. She'd seen the whole thing and let out a sharp laugh. "Good luck with *that*, Jane," she said. "He's never going to like you."

"I don't know, Dagmar," Captain Superlative said. "I'm pretty sure that Tyler likes everyone."

Dagmar pointed a manicured finger at me. "I see what you're doing. That's not how things work in this school."

It was true. Things had worked differently—until now.

I shrugged. "Have a good day, Dagmar."

"Yes," Captain Superlative said. "Good luck on the test! Or, as they say in the theatre, 'Break a leg!'"

Swallowing a scream of frustration, Dagmar turned her head up and stalked down the hall. April—who I'd completely forgotten was there—followed, waving to me and calling out, "Thanks, Janey!"

So she still remembered my name after all.

"Well, Janey," Captain Superlative said, when we were at last alone. "How do you feel about your first test of bravery?"

"Like I'm going to be sick," I said, shaking my head a little bit. "I can't believe we just did that to Dagmar Hagen."

"We didn't do anything to Dagmar," Captain Superlative said. "People made their own choices."

"It could really come back to explode in our faces."

"Maybe," she said. "But maybe not. Either way, it'll be fun finding out what happens next."

"Yeah," I said uneasily. "Fun."

I thought about Tyler's lip, the way he'd smiled at me. The knot of anxiety in the pit of my stomach started to loosen.

Maybe this *would* be fun after all.

Captain Superlative draped an arm around my shoulders

and we started down the hall. She talked about our next great heroic scheme—something to do with doors—but I have to admit, I was only half listening. I looked from side to side, at the banks of lockers where other kids were putting away their coats, chatting with each other, scanning their new study guides. Some of them glanced up at us with smiles or waves. These were some of the same kids who'd formed a bubble around me back in third grade, who'd left me feeling isolated and without a friend in the world. I guess they'd changed since then.

Or maybe I had.

# 13

**"Sorry I'm late," Captain Superlative** said, before curling up her fist and coughing into it. She was still in her coat, cheeks flushed pink from the morning air. It was Tuesday, and the lunch bell had just sounded. I'd spent most of the morning feeling like a bundle of nerve endings, ready at any second to become yet another target for Dagmar, but there'd been no sign of her today. Out sick, apparently. The panic had slowly started to melt away by the time Captain Superlative found me.

"You okay?" I asked her.

"Yeah." She coughed again, but then took a deep breath and nodded, straightening up. "Just had to miss class. Family stuff." She nodded toward a bank of lockers before slipping her arm over my shoulders. "C'mon." She led me down the hall. "Let me drop off my stuff, then let's head to the cafeteria. We've got a job to do."

It was nice to have a friend waiting to walk with me.

"Hey, thanks for the study guide, Captain!" someone said, coming out of the classroom behind me.

"You're welcome!" she said, waving in no particular direction.

A chorus of follow-up thank-yous sounded off. Yesterday's test had been brutal, and a lot of the trick questions had been in the study guide. Who could remember that the ancient Athenian marketplace was called an *agora*?

Well. I could. *Now.*

Captain Superlative dropped her bag in front of a locker and started to turn the lock. "How did it go manning the doors this morning?" I'd agreed to hold them open for any teachers who came by with their hands full, just the way I'd seen her do it the day I'd followed her.

"Fine," I said.

"I'll bet those doors were no match for you!"

"They were just doors."

"Never *just*."

"What did your family have you doing?"

Before she could answer, a math worksheet drifted to my feet. "Look," Captain Superlative said, pointing down to it. "Quick, there's a citizen in need."

I laughed and picked it up. When I stood up, Tyler Jeffries was standing smack in front of me. Again. Two days in a row felt like winning the lottery. It felt like winning the lottery *twice*. "Thanks," he said, taking the paper from my rigid hand.

"No problem."

"Hey. It's Jane, right?"

"Yeah. Uh, you can call me Janey."

"Janey, the Greek goddess of social studies."

"I don't know about that. . . ."

"Are you kidding? Without you, I would have said Feta Cheese was the name of the temple at the top of the Acropolis."

"You think with your stomach a lot."

Tyler barely had to pause before he made a comeback. "In my defense, food is delicious," he said.

"I guess it is."

"Also, I'm a ham."

"I can't argue with that," I said, remembering his football performance at Sunset Ridge Park. "Although I should probably point out that ham is also a food."

"Is it?"

"Last time I checked."

He gave us a dimpled smile. "Oh well." He shrugged. "Thanks again, Captain Superlative. Janey."

I couldn't remember the rest of the walk to the cafeteria until I felt Captain Superlative nudge me with her elbow. "Janey?"

"What?"

"What's the matter with you?

"Tyler Jeffries knows my name."

"Why does that surprise you?"

Because he was Tyler Jeffries.

The school cafeteria was a large square-shaped room with enormous gray and white tiles arranged in a checkerboard pattern on the floor. The sort of tiles that you would play "hot lava" on, skipping from white tile to white tile, pretending that the gray ones would melt your shoes. Of course, that was only a game. But the room had always promised danger of a different kind. It wasn't quite the no-man's-land that the hallways were—there were teachers milling around the perimeter—but it was still a place where Dagmar held court, where a word from her could make or break your spirit. Still a place where you could get burned. Even if she was out today, I still felt my throat tighten a little as we walked inside. This would be another test of my new resolve.

Captain Superlative pulled a pair of brown paper bags out of her backpack, holding one of them out to me. "What's this?" I asked.

"Mints," she replied.

I opened the bag, the smell hitting me. There were probably two hundred in there, all nestled in their own crinkly cellophane wrapping. They looked like jewels, glittering in the harsh, fluorescent light. "Okay. What are we doing with mints?"

"The eighth graders have a science test today. Why don't you go offer them to the kids who haven't taken it yet?" she said. "They say that peppermint improves your memory."

I'd heard the same thing. My dad insisted that it was a myth spread by the peppermint manufacturers' super-secret society—obviously headquartered in a hollowed-out volcano—to increase sales to gullible middle school students. "You don't really believe that, do you?"

She shrugged. "Does it matter? Some people do. And some people just like mints."

Okay. If I signed on for this ride, I was going to take it. I gave her a nod, grabbed the bag, and started to walk from table to table. Deerwood Park Middle School had long rectangular tables that stretched across the room, with benches attached to either side. There were no assigned seats, but the one you took in sixth grade usually became your seat for life. That's just the way it worked. For the last year and a half, I'd always sat at the very end of the bench of the very last table, closest to the door. Not exactly alone, but definitely isolated. I didn't know what kind of reception to expect. It wasn't that bad, though. Not bad at all. Everyone I stopped for took a mint. I got some smiles, a couple thank-yous. Several kids even thanked me by name. And not Jane. But *Janey*. Or, as my dad would have put it, *Janey!*

"Is it true, what they're saying?" a seventh grader asked me as she took a mint from the bag.

"What are they saying?"

"That you and Captain Superlative humiliated Dagmar Hagen, and there's a video of the whole thing online?"

"What? No. Nothing like that."

"Oh." I couldn't tell if the girl was disappointed or skeptical. But she gave me a funny look before I moved on to the next table.

I spotted Paige walking into the cafeteria, carefully balancing all of her textbooks and what looked like a dictionary in her arms. "Janey," she said with a smile as I approached her.

"Mint?" I asked her, holding out the bag.

"Thanks." She tucked her books under her arm and took one, twirling the end of the wrapper between her fingers. I lingered, watching her and watching the way she chewed on her lip. "You're sitting with Captain Superlative today?" she said, after a moment.

"Yeah. Over there." I gestured to the table on top of which Captain Superlative was sitting with her feet on the bench, handing out mints. "You want to sit with us?"

"Sure."

"C'mon."

We made our way over to the table, but just before we got there, Paige glanced at me out of the corner of her eye. "You know what that means, right?"

"What?"

"Sitting with me and Captain Superlative?"

"It means that I'm with you," I said.

She smiled slightly. "Good."

"Hi, Paige," Captain Superlative said as Paige dropped her things on the table.

"What are you doing?" I asked, nodding to the dictionary.

Paige laughed. "Writing a song."

"What's it called?" Captain Superlative asked.

"I think it's called 'The Girl Next Door,'" Paige said.

"You think?"

"I'm not sure yet. Songs have a way of deciding these things for you, once you finish them."

"Let's hear it."

"I'm still working on the tune. It'll probably go something like this." Paige closed her eyes and hummed for a moment, before she actually sang:

*The demons are people*
*And the people are demons*

*And the scales of justice*
*Will never be even*

*When life gets you down*
*The demons make it worse*
*Of all the things I've learned*
*This lesson was my first*

I was astonished. Paige's voice was so sweet, so beautiful. Like birdsong. It hung in the air even after she was done. And I wasn't sure whether to applaud or cry or what. Captain Superlative frowned though, tilting her head. "Why's it called 'The Girl Next Door'?"

Paige shook her head. "I don't know yet. I'll figure it out."

The rest of the day was more of the same. Between classes, Captain Superlative and I walked the halls. I spent my free period in the library with her, going from table to table, offering help to the sixth graders on the material that I'd already learned. Captain Superlative was better with social studies and math, but I actually knew more of the answers to their questions about science and language arts.

"We complement each other nicely," she said as we left one table of grateful kids studying for a quiz.

"I guess we do."

After the final bell, I skipped out of my class, racing to the front entrance. There were two sets of double doors, and now there were two of us to (wo)man them. Captain Superlative took the left. I took the right. We opened them when there were people who needed to get through. Closed them to keep out the cold air when there weren't.

"Getting twice as much work done!" Captain Superlative said.

"Yeah." It was true.

"You show that door who's boss! Give it a good 'boom' next time."

I laughed. "I'm not going to do that."

"Give it a try, it'll be fun. Watch!" She opened the door for a pair of eighth graders. "Boom!"

I shook my head.

"Try it, Janey!"

It was so silly, but when I opened the door for Mr. Collins, I shouted, "Kapow!"

"That's the spirit!"

Tuesday ended without any disasters. I found myself feeling giddy with excitement when I told my dad about my adventures. And proud. Proud of myself, even if I'd only done the little things.

He was proud of me too. I could tell because he said so—and because he decided we should go to the movies, even though it was a school night.

"Not that superheroes should expect rewards," he warned me as we got into the car.

"I know, Dad."

"They're not in it for the money or the product endorsements."

I pictured Captain Superlative's face on a box of cereal and couldn't stop laughing.

---

Dagmar was back the next day. I didn't see her all morning, but I felt her presence everywhere. There were whispers in the halls. And this time, kids stopped to whisper to me. "She's in a bad mood," Kevin Marks said, with a conspiratorial glance to one side. "Nasty black eye. I think she took a soccer ball to the face."

"That doesn't sound fun," I said.

"Nope," he agreed, wheeling himself through the auditorium door I was holding open. "Thanks, Janey!"

"She didn't get hit in the face," April said, when I picked up a calculator that had fallen out of her bag. "She wasn't even at practice yesterday. Her mom took her to a spa! You know, one of those super-fancy, fabulous places where you can get all kinds of cool, weird treatments that clean out your pores and stuff."

I had no idea what she meant, really. But I'd never heard of someone coming back from a luxury spa with a black eye before. "That's weird," I said.

April shrugged. "That's Dagmar. Thanks, Janey." And off she went, shoving the calculator back into her bag. Right before she reached the bend in the hallway, though, she turned to look over her shoulder at me. "Hey, Janey?"

"Yeah?"

"Why don't we hang out anymore?"

"I . . ." How did I put that into words? *Because you started treating me like a freak after my mother died?* Did she not even remember? She'd been the one to end our friendship.

Hadn't she?

"I miss you," she continued. "That's all."

And she was gone.

"Believe me, it's not from a spa," Paige said, when I sat down at her table during lunch, recounting the story with more than a little confusion.

"What happened?"

Paige frowned slightly, closing her dictionary over a piece of loose-leaf paper with the latest verses of what I assumed was her song. I saw the words *people* and *demons*, anyway. "It's kind of complicated. And I'm not sure I should say. How much do you know about Dagmar's family?"

"I know that her mother is some kind of sophisticated and fashion—"

A shadow fell over us.

There was Dagmar, as golden as ever. She wore a red dress with a gold thread pattern in the fabric. Her curls were loose, falling around her neck and shoulders. They *almost* pulled the attention away from the heavily caked makeup around her black eye. Almost.

Her gaze zeroed in on Paige, the way it had a thousand times before. But this was the thousand-and-first time. Things were different now. I put my hands down on the table and stood up, partly blocking her view. I could do that now that I wasn't just air. I was a solid person, with a shape and with substance.

And a mission.

"Hi, Dagmar," I said.

"Dagmar! You're back!" Captain Superlative came loping over to us from another table, where she'd been helping some sixth graders with math.

Dagmar whirled around, first looking at her, then back at me.

"Do you want to sit with us?" Captain Superlative asked, gesturing to an empty stretch of bench beside Paige. "We could talk or something."

I smiled.

Powerless rage flickered in Dagmar's eyes. There was a hunger in her, an aching need to rip someone's throat out. I saw her fingers twitch. Would she do it? The cafeteria got quiet as more kids turned to look at us. Dagmar thrived on an audience. But this particular audience was made up of witnesses. I hadn't realized how much goodwill Captain Superlative had built in the school so quickly.

Dagmar felt it too, I think.

"Hey, is there a problem over there?" Tyler and a few of his friends, two tables away, had turned to watch with everyone else.

Dagmar's eyes flicked back and forth, from Tyler to me and Captain Superlative. Angrily, she slammed her palm on the top of the table, shaking our cartons of milk. With a snarl, she turned around, stalking out of the cafeteria. Not even April made to follow her. We all just watched her through the glass as she blazed down the hall and disappeared.

Captain Superlative frowned a little, shaking her head. She seemed lost in her own thoughts, until someone across the room dropped a fork and startled her back to the present. It had gotten incredibly quiet.

How many times had we seen the story go the other way? All too often it was Dagmar who sent someone else running from the room, fighting back tears at a witty comeback or the crushing pain of humiliation. It had never been like this before. *Never.* I think we knew that this was an important moment, even if no one was prepared to say as much. Maybe because we were still in it. It's hard to reflect on a moment you're still living inside of.

The fork broke the silence. And the cafeteria returned to normal, everyone chatting and laughing and joking around.

Only Paige was quiet. She looked like she wanted to say something, but when I looked over at her, inviting her to speak, she shook her head and went back to working on her song.

I let it pass without another thought.

It was another moment.

I'd figure it out, eventually.

# 14

**"You should draw something on** Ms. Hinton's board," Captain Superlative said to me one afternoon.

Three weeks, and what felt like a lifetime, had gone by. It was more than a little surreal to go from being part of absolutely zero clubs to being a member of the most exclusive one in school. But being with Captain Superlative meant a new adventure every day. We had our regular duties, of course. We (wo)manned the doors in the mornings and afternoons, teaching them—those monsters, as Captain Superlative called them—a lesson they would never forget. We helped pick up books and papers and pencils in the bustling hallways. We became Paige's personal hallway escorts. We passed out mints in the cafeteria every time we knew about a big test. We even helped scrub the dry-erase boards at the end of the day.

We were in Ms. Hinton's room when Captain Superlative made the suggestion. I turned and gave her a bewildered look. "What?"

"I've seen the way you doodle," she said, standing up on her tiptoes. She could just barely reach the top of the board with the very end of the eraser. "You're really good."

I reached over with my own eraser to help her with the high parts. "You think so?"

"Yeah."

I bit down on the inside of my cheek. "What would I even draw?"

Captain Superlative shrugged. "How about a moose?"

"Why a moose?"

"Why not?"

"I've never drawn a moose before."

"Give it a shot."

The moose ended up looking more like a lopsided egg with two hands sticking out of it, but Ms. Hinton said she loved it anyway.

The weeks went by and Captain Superlative continued to push me to pick a superhero name—which made me think more about her name. *Superlative*. It came from deep inside her, a need to be bigger, better, bestest. Our regular duties were just that to her. Regular. "There has to be more," she would mutter, more to herself than to me.

"Like what?" I would ask.

*"Something."*

Our work started to move beyond Deerwood Park Middle School. Captain Superlative almost always had something important after school. But on the days when she had time, she'd walk home with me. It started with one of those walks. Someone had tossed an empty plastic bottle on the sidewalk and I accidentally kicked it. It went skipping down the sidewalk, turning end over end with a few hollow clanks before it fell on its side and rolled toward the curb. Captain Superlative stopped and scooped it up. I wrinkled my nose. "Ew."

"It's okay," she said. "I've got my gloves." For a moment, she just stared at the bottle, as if it held the secret of the universe somewhere. Then the moment seemed to pass and we continued walking.

A few squares of sidewalk later, she stopped again, this time to grab a crushed tin can from the gutter beside the curb. I shook my head. "What are you doing?"

"I'll drop these in the recycling bin when I get home," she said. "The town is a citizen too! It's not just people who need our help."

"That's gross."

"You're just intimidated."

"Intimidated?"

She puffed out her chest a little, eyes gleaming underneath her mask. "Yeah. Because you know that you can't pick up more than me before we get to your apartment."

I immediately knew what she was doing. And I wasn't about to let her goad me into it. "I have longer arms," I replied with a dismissive shrug. "I can hold more stuff." And I put a firm nod on the end of the sentence. To indicate it was the end.

It wasn't.

"Prove it."

She went loping ahead, snatching a flattened french fries

box. She looked over her shoulder at me, but I just shook my head. "I'm not playing that game."

"Yes you are!" She shot ahead again, this time to grab another crushed can. "Come on, Janey. Catch up! I'm ahead of you."

"I'm not doing it!" I said, cupping my hands around my mouth. I had to press the corners of my lips together to keep from smiling, though.

"You can go faster than that!" She lurched forward for an abandoned coffee cup with the name *Mark* written on the side.

"Nope!"

"Come on, Janey!"

"I will not." But I could feel it. I could feel the urge to chase after her building up inside of me, tingling up my legs and getting my heart racing like a drumbeat.

"Come on!"

It was too delicious to resist. I followed her down the sidewalk as she half goaded, half encouraged me, clapping the bottle against the coffee cup. Faster and faster. The wind swept my hair back from my face, exposing my neck and shoulders. With every step, I felt myself becoming lighter. The world had relinquished its hold on me, and I knew that any second I'd be in the stratosphere, bound for the stars.

*So this is what it feels like to fly.*

Just like that, the world outside the school was equally under our protection. We'd swing by the supermarket and help people load groceries (my idea). We'd stop to scrape up the ice along the walkway (hers). Or we might brush the fine and powdery snow of a fresh flurry off parked cars (both of us, really). And always, we stayed true to Captain Superlative's mission to cheer people up. One day, we stopped just to watch Tyler and his friends play football in the park, her cheering for one team, me cheering for the other. (I miraculously ended up cheering for Tyler's team.)

Once—although I'd invited her many times before—Captain Superlative stayed at my apartment for dinner. My dad was falling over himself to be a good host. He told a thousand jokes. He and Captain Superlative struck up an animated conversation about their favorite superheroes (my dad liked Batman, Captain Superlative liked Hawkgirl, but they both agreed that Spider-Man was terrific). He made all of his best recipes. Most amazing of all, he even excused me from dish duty, insisting that the two of us should go hide out in my room.

"Spend some quality time in the Fortress of Solitude," he said, shooing us out of the kitchen with a dishrag. "I'm sure you have plots to plot and schemes to scheme."

I had no idea what that meant.

But Captain Superlative had the answer. As soon as I closed the door, her eyes widened beneath her mask and she suggested we cut out valentines for everyone in the seventh grade. It was no fun when you didn't get a valentine on Valentine's Day. We owed it to our fellow citizens to spread the love.

We got busy cutting and drawing.

"I don't remember how it works," she said, sitting with the soles of her feet pressed together on the end of my bed, cutting a heart out of some red construction paper. Selina was nestled in between her legs, purring loud enough for me to hear.

"I say the word," I said. "And then you have to come up with a word that starts with the same letter and means something similar."

"I think you'd pretty much beat me every time," she said, shaking her head.

"I could start you off easy?"

"I don't know."

"How about *peaceful*?"

"Peaceful . . . pleasant?"

"That's a good one!" I said, giving her a grin. "Then I would say something like *pacifying*."

"Is that really a word?"

"Of course. You've never heard it before?"

"English isn't my first language, Janey."

"It isn't?"

She shook her head, setting the heart onto the pile by her side. My job was to draw something on each heart, then put it into another pile. I couldn't think of anything clever to draw, mostly just valentine-y stuff. Kissy lips and flowers. Later, we'd decorate them with glitter and stickers. My yearbook from last year sat open on my desk, with the pictures and names of all of our classmates, so that we could address them personally. That was the most important part, Captain Superlative told me.

As I started to draw a silhouette of a cupid with a bow and arrow, I watched Captain Superlative work. Of course, unmasking her as Caitlyn Li meant that I knew she was

Chinese, but somehow I'd forgotten. She wasn't a person, not really. She was a force of nature. And a force of nature had no first language. It spoke every language without saying a word.

I wondered what else I didn't know about Captain Superlative.

"You know what we should do?" she asked.

"What?"

"We should—" She broke off suddenly, coughing. "We should—" She couldn't stop coughing. Just like when she laughed, she put her whole body into it, shoulders bunching up, head dropping into her hands.

"Are you okay?"

Her face turned bright pink under the mask. "Excuse—" *Cough.* "Me—" *Cough.* "A second." She shot out of my room, crossed the hall to the bathroom, and slammed the door, leaving Selina in a confused pile on the floor. She looked up at me and mewed pitifully. I just shrugged.

I heard the sink running under the continued sound of her coughing fit. Slowly, she got the cough under control. Another minute or two and she came back, face still pink and damp, but smiling all the same.

"What was that?" I asked.

She shook her head. "Nothing."

"Are you sure?"

It didn't sound like nothing.

"Yeah. And hey, I had an idea." She sank down on the bed again. "We should put a little picture by each person's name, representing one of the clubs they list in the yearbook. That would really personalize it."

"I don't know," I said, wrinkling up my nose. "What do you draw that represents the quiz bowl team?"

"You're the artist," she said. I liked that she called me that. "You tell me."

I considered it a moment. "I could draw one of those funny graduation hats. What are they called?"

She coughed into her fist. "Mortarboards?"

"Yeah!"

"Brilliant, Janey!" She grinned. Selina hopped back up on the bed, tentatively sniffing at Captain Superlative, like she wasn't sure if she was ready to forgive her or not. Captain Superlative held a palm out to her, letting her sniff it.

"Do you think we have time for that?" I asked.

"Sure. It's a million years until Valentine's Day."

"It's only a week or two, at this point."

Wow. What had happened to January? It had just flown away from me.

"I'll tell you what," Captain Superlative said, running her fingers along the fur between Selina's ears. "I'll take charge of all the glitter and stickers and names. That way you can focus on just the drawing part."

"All right. Sounds good to me." And way better than drawing kissy lips and flowers.

"That's because we're a great team!"

"The best team," I said with a laugh.

"There's no better team in the history of the universe."

"Except for Batman and Robin," my dad said from the other side of the door.

That made us laugh. A lot. We were seized with fits so wild and uncontrolled that Selina gave up on waiting for us to calm down and indignantly jumped from the bed to my desk with narrowed green eyes. The look on her face made us laugh harder. We collapsed into the paper hearts, which scattered like autumn leaves. We might have laughed for the rest of time, except for the fact that our frail human bodies needed to breathe. Before too long, we were both exhausted, coughing and gasping to catch our breaths.

"Can I tell you something funny?" I asked her, shifting my weight to lie down across the head of my bed.

"Sure." She flopped over the foot, a few more hearts fluttering to the ground. Selina forgot all about us, chasing after a heart and disappearing under my bed.

"I don't think I've ever been as happy as I am right now."

"Good," she said, starting to cough again. "Life." Each word was a struggle, coming out like a wheeze. "Is. Too short. To be sad. All. The time."

"And anything less than superlative," I reminded her. I'd never forgotten that somehow. Those incredible, powerful words. When I closed my eyes, I could still see her in the living room that night, changing the way I looked at everything, urging me to be superlative.

"That too."

I stared up at the ceiling. "Superlative," I said softly, enjoying the way the word felt in my mouth.

"Sensational," Captain Superlative said.

Oh, challenge accepted. "Superb," I countered.

"Supreme."

"Spectacular."

She faltered. And then said, "Super-de-duper!"

I shot up ramrod straight. "That is not a word!"

"Is too," she replied, giving me a sly grin as she sat up.

"It is not!"

"It is *now*!"

"Don't argue with the superhero," my dad said from the other side of the door.

"Stop listening in, Dad!"

"He's right," Captain Superlative said, thrusting out her chin.

I grabbed a handful of the paper hearts to my side and threw them at her. They didn't quite have the same impact as a snowball. They drifted around her, spinning and twirling. One or two landed in her wig. A few fell on her arms and chest. One managed to land almost perfectly over her actual heart. I found myself thinking... *That's what Captain Superlative is.* Forgetting the mask and the cape and the wig and the catchphrase and all that other stuff... *Captain Superlative is love.*

But just as the thought formed in my head, she let out a peal of laughter. "This means war!" She grabbed a handful of hearts and threw them back at me. Not one to be bombarded or outdone, I started throwing them back, and between the two of us, we made a pretty fantastic mess.

A superlative mess, you might even say.

I guess wars are always messy. But this was a special kind of war. A wonderful kind of war. A war fought with love.

# 15

**It felt so easy. All these little things** that I'd thought were meaningless? They all added up. They really did. And the more I noticed people I could stop to help, the more I noticed something else.

I generally met up with Captain Superlative in the library, between fourth and fifth period. I got there first on Monday and went inside to our usual table to wait for her. Another big test was coming up—this time in Math—so we were going to hand out mints, I assumed. I perched myself on the corner of the table, staring out at the wall of glass that overlooked the hallway. Kids were going back and forth. In the last few weeks, a lot of the girls and even some of the boys had started wearing red high-top sneakers, just like Captain Superlative. There were two major camps now, one for red high-tops, the other for Blue Shoes. When

Tyler made a joke about combining the two and wearing *purple* high-tops, a tiny third camp popped up. It was a little bit like the end of *The Sneetches*. No one could keep track of what was "in" or "out" anymore. And, really, no one seemed to care too much. Especially without Dagmar to dictate policy.

She'd been suspiciously quiet as of late.

Among the sea of bobbing heads, I spotted Paige, carrying her books like always. She *really* needed a bag. I grabbed a felt-tip marker and I made a note to myself on the back of my hand to go through the hall closet and see if I could find one of my old ones for her. Predictably, one of her books fell off the stack in front of her. I started to slide off the table, eager to run out and pick it up for her, but someone else beat me to it.

It wasn't Captain Superlative.

Tyler was passing Paige, going the other way. He stopped and smiled at her, leaning over to pick up the book and a couple sheets of paper.

It was like watching a movie. An old silent movie that was all faces and no words.

He seemed to ask her if she was okay.

Paige was startled, flustered that the most popular boy in school was talking to her, let alone helping her.

Tyler was blissfully oblivious to her astonishment. He said something. I was an expert at watching his lips, and I'm pretty sure it was her name.

She clearly couldn't believe that he knew it.

He set the book back on top of her stack. And then he asked her something about what was written on her paper.

One of her songs, no doubt. Paige looked bashful, the way she always did when her songs came up.

Tyler returned the pages to her. He turned to one side, saw me—and waved.

It was maybe thirty seconds, at most. But it was also a new lifetime. Paige watched Tyler walk away, unsure if it had happened. But it had. We were both witnesses. She saw me through the glass and mouthed, *Tyler Jeffries!*

I smiled.

We were making a difference. We really were making a difference.

On the Tuesday before the Valentine's Day dance, another impossible thing happened. Between sixth and seventh period, I went looking for Paige. I'd dug out one of my old book bags. It wasn't anything special. It was kind of plain and green. But I figured it would be better than having to lug around her books in her arms. It would leave her less vulnerable too. Plus, green was her favorite color. I was sure Captain Superlative would approve. My dad certainly did. He dubbed me "Super J" and insisted that we go out to Sunset Ridge to brush up on my "swordplay" skills, using two old and yellowing plastic baseball bats.

I spotted her coming out of the girls' bathroom and was about to make my way over, but suddenly someone else shouted, "Paige!"

It was April. She came down the hall, a red comet in her soccer uniform and red sneakers, silky blond hair streaming behind her. I couldn't remember ever seeing her talk to Paige before. I couldn't even remember her *looking* at Paige.

"Hey, Paige," she said.

"Hi." Paige's reply was tentative, testing the waters.

If April noticed, she certainly didn't show it. "I love those jeans!" she said. "They're so cute."

Paige's jeans seemed like jeans to me. They were a pale, faded blue, hugging her hips and fraying a little bit around her heels. Nothing special. But then again, I'd never really had much of an interest in clothes. April, on the other hand, had been an expert in clothing since our days of playing dress-up in the basement of my old house. It was only because of her that I knew not to wear brown pants with a blue purse.

Paige glanced down at them, a little bit self-conscious. "They're my sister's," she said, muttering to the earth.

"Well, your sister has great taste."

This wasn't the way the scene was supposed to play out. April was deviating from the script. The popular girl didn't compliment the outsider. But then, the popular girl didn't wear red high-tops either. Paige looked up with a timid smile. "She does?" she asked.

"Yeah."

"Thanks."

April smoothed her hair back behind her ear. "Heading to Gym?"

"Yeah."

"I'll walk with you." And she reached out, taking a couple of books off of Paige's pile. She didn't throw them to the ground or spit on them. She didn't kick them. She didn't rip up any of Paige's assignments. "Let me give you a hand," she said instead, tucking them under her arm.

"Thank you!"

"Sure." And suddenly the two of them were walking away, following the flow of kids to the gym. "So where did your sister get those jeans?"

"I'm not sure, really."

Had April changed? Or had I misjudged her? Had I been the one to cut her out of my life after third grade? Had I lost sight of who she was, assuming that her loyalty to Dagmar defined her? It was something to think about. But either way, she was being surprisingly nice to Paige now.

And that's what it was all adding up to. What the Captain did? Other kids started to do. As I watched it all happening, swirling around me like some kind of cyclone of change, I failed to notice something else that was happening.

On Wednesday afternoon, I manned the front doors—now decorated with pink and red hearts for the Valentine's Day dance—after school. By myself. It was the middle of the week and Captain Superlative had been strangely absent. It was a school. Kids missed class sometimes. But three days in a row were making me uneasy. I'd gotten so used to our routines that it felt like something was missing every time I arrived and she didn't.

Like I was facing down a villain (or door) by myself.

I was just a sidekick. I wasn't ready for more than that yet.

I opened the door for Ms. Hinton, who was carrying a box filled with papers. "Thank you, Jane," she said, offering me a smile. "Great job on that test, by the way. I'm very proud of you." I'd gotten a solid A—my first ever in her class—thanks to the study guides. Quite the turnaround for an average B student.

Once she was outside, unsteadily making her way across the crunching snow, I closed the doors with a soft "Kablam!" and became aware of laughing.

On the other side of the entry hall, a group of kids from the school play were standing in a huddle, like football players making plans. Tyler was there, at the center of it all. His friends were snickering, one of them nudging him in the ribs with an elbow while another whacked him on the shoulder with a winter cap.

They kept looking at me.

I did my best to ignore it. I opened the door for Kevin, who was finally out of the wheelchair and wobbling on crutches. "Be careful!" I called after him, eyeing the icy walkway nervously.

Two sixth graders scurried over, flanking Kevin's sides, their hands ready to catch him if he slipped. They yapped at him and followed along like eager puppies.

I smiled in satisfaction and closed the door, nearly walking right into Tyler, who appeared behind me.

"Whoa!"

"Hey, Janey."

A couple of his friends started laughing again. One of them—the eighth-grade girl cast as Mrs. Potts—gave a kid in the chorus a wink.

"Hi," I said, my eyebrows drawing together.

What was so funny?

Tyler took a glove out of his pocket, twisting it between his hands. "How are you today?" he asked.

Two eighth graders balancing a papier-mâché volcano came down the hall. I put a hand on Tyler's shoulder, gently shoving him aside so I could open the door for them and they could pass without knocking into him. "I'm good," I said, once they were through. Almost as an afterthought, I called, "Have a good afternoon, citizens!" It felt like something Captain Superlative would have said. Although she would have made it sound better.

Where *was* she?

Tyler moved back toward me, his knuckles beginning to turn white as he continued to wind the glove around his hands. "So I was thinking. And not with my stomach this time."

"What?"

"You know, how you said—"

"Oh, right."

"Thanks again, by the way. I actually pulled an A-minus on the test. And I only mentioned gyros once."

"I'm glad to hear it."

"Anyway," he said, looking to one side. "I wanted to ask you something about the Valentine's Day da—"

"Listen," I interrupted, my agitation getting the better of me. "Have you seen Captain Superlative?"

"No. I don't think so. I'm pretty sure she wasn't in science class this morning." The corners of his lips lifted up into another smile. "It would be hard to miss her, right?"

"Yeah," I said. "It would."

He shrugged. "I mean, you know, she's been sick. Guess she didn't make it to school today."

But she hadn't made it Tuesday. Or Monday. "That doesn't sound like her," I said, the creep of unease rising in my chest.

"No?"

"Not really."

"No rest for the righteous, huh?"

"Something like that."

Behind him, Tyler's friends started laughing again. A sixth-grade girl in the chorus touched the back of her hand to her forehead and slumped against the side of the boy playing Chip. "Yeah." Tyler cast a sidelong glance at them and they all immediately shut up, snapping stiffly to attention like soldiers. "Well. So, anyway." He turned back to me. "I wanted to ask you if you'd like to go—"

"Maybe I should stop by her house," I said, more thinking out loud than actually talking to him.

"What?"

"Captain Superlative's house."

"Oh." And then he chuckled a little. "I guess you would know where her secret base of operations is?"

"It's really not that big a secret."

It was pretty certain that everyone in the school, at this point, knew that Captain Superlative was Caitlyn Li. Or at least everyone in the seventh grade. But there was some kind of unspoken agreement that no one talked about it. Even the teachers liked calling her Captain Superlative. Sometimes just Captain.

And our principal, Dr. Wallace, was playing along too.

Tyler shrugged. "Yeah, but I like the mystery."

"Yeah." I nodded slightly. "Yeah, I think I'll do that."

"Do what?"

"Go to her house."

"Oh," Tyler said, taking a few steps back from the door. "You never give up, do you?"

"I guess not."

"Me neither."

"Hey, Ty!" one of Tyler's friends said. "We're going to be late for rehearsal."

"Yeah!" another one said. "Mr. Hoffman will make us drop and do fifty."

I looked up at him in surprise. "Fifty? Fifty what? Push-ups?"

"Nah." Tyler grinned. "Fifty jazz squares."

"What?"

"Jazz squares." He did a quick little dance step, his feet moving around the perimeter of an invisible square. The other kids in the play seemed to find this hilarious. "See?" He held out his hands to either side, fingers splayed and wiggling.

"Oh."

"Come on, Twinkle Toes!" another kid from the play called, dropping to give Tyler a balletic curtsy. A couple of the others in the group hooted, copying him.

Tyler waved them off. "Listen," he said to me. "I want to ask you about something, okay? Think you'll have a few minutes to talk tomorrow?"

"Yeah, okay," I said.

"Promise?"

"Sure. Sure."

"Great." A step back. "Well." Another step back. "See you later, Janey." He waved at me, turning around to rejoin his friends. One threw an arm over his shoulder. All of them seemed to be in hysterics again over something. I didn't know what, but they continued to laugh and laugh as they followed him down the hall.

"Are you sure Hoffman cast him in the right part?" someone asked.

"Yeah," another said. "Gaston isn't supposed to strike out."

"I thought you were a method actor, Ty."

"Smooth going, lover boy."

"Yeah, yeah," Tyler said. "Just you wait."

"On the edge of my seat, hot stuff."

They were making fun of him. Tyler was taking it in stride, like always. And I barely noticed any of it.

When Tyler Jeffries had fallen from being the first thing on my mind, I can't begin to guess. But he had, and now I was consumed with thoughts of Captain Superlative. If this had been a comic book, I would have supposed some villain had tied her to a rocket or the train tracks or a nuclear bomb. But this wasn't a comic book. And I couldn't imagine she was in any of those places. I didn't know where she was at all.

That scared me.

# 16

**In five weeks Captain Superlative had** become my whole world, but I hadn't been to the Li house since the day I followed her and her parents home from the hospital. It wasn't for lack of trying, though. I was *always* asking to hang out after school. She was *always* deflecting my question with one excuse or another. She was busy. She had a headache. She had to be "somewhere." When I asked her what she was doing, she smiled and said, "Supersecret superhero stuff. You'll find out when you graduate from being a sidekick."

Not exactly a concrete answer.

So the Li house was uncharted territory for me.

I stood at the spot where the sidewalk met the driveway, staring up at the small, squat redbrick home. There were two windows over the garage. The curtains—an inexplicable neon shade of green—were drawn. I knew that Captain

Superlative was in that room. I felt her presence on the other side of the glass, just as sure as I felt it whenever she was standing behind my shoulder.

But why? Why was she in a place shut out of the light, instead of zooming through the halls, her arms raised above her head, flying?

Why wasn't she with me?

Each step I took toward the welcome mat on the front stoop felt heavy, like a part of me didn't want to take the next step. The dark, weighty dread felt like lifting a million pounds when I raised my finger to press the doorbell.

The cheeriness of the chime was out of place.

After a moment, Mrs. Li opened the front door. She was just like I remembered her, wearing a pencil skirt and a clip in her glossy black hair. The only difference was that she was wearing a strange pair of slippers instead of heels. Her dark eyes peered out at me, over the tops of a tiny pair of glasses.

"Hello," she said. She had a strong accent, and that same firm tenderness I remembered from the hospital.

"Hi."

A pause. She waited patiently, but when I didn't speak, she asked, "May I help you?"

"Uh, I was looking for Captain Su . . . I mean . . . Caitlyn." It felt unnatural to call her that.

"Oh." There was something inside of that "oh" that sounded fearful.

"I'm a friend of hers," I said quickly. "Janey. Jane Silverman."

"Yes. She has mentioned you. Quite a bit." Her smile was hollow, not quite reaching her eyes.

"She wasn't in school today, so I wondered—"

"Today was a bad day."

I stood there, blinking, uncomprehending. "Bad day?"

"The whole week has been bad."

"Bad week? What do you mean?" Somehow I didn't think Captain Superlative was capable of having a bad day, let alone a bad week. Not even a bad *second*.

"The treatments have been making her tired."

"Treatments?" The word didn't make sense. I mean, I knew it *was* a word. My dad used it plenty, talking about medications and procedures for his animals. But what did it have to do with Captain Superlative?

Mrs. Li pursed her lips. "She did not tell you?"

"Tell me what?" I hadn't seen her all week. Hadn't heard from her.

"I think, perhaps, you should come back tomorrow and—"

"What's going on?" I didn't mean to interrupt. And I didn't mean for my voice to suddenly get high and tight.

"I am not sure if I should be the one to tell you, Jane."

What did that even mean? "Tell me what?"

She sighed softly, rubbing her eye underneath one lens of her glasses as she let out a few words in what I assumed was Chinese. After a second or two, she seemed to make a decision, stepping out of the doorway and gesturing for me to come inside. Beside the door, under a gurgling little fountain with stones and bamboo shoots, I saw a neat row of shoes and boots, including Captain Superlative's red high-top sneakers. Mrs. Li didn't say anything, but she nodded toward the line of shoes, indicating that I should take mine off.

Numbly, I took off my shoes and lined them up next to the red high-tops.

The Li house was all straight lines and even spaces, from the way the art was hung on the walls to the arrangement of the furniture. She led me through a living room with carefully placed furniture to an immaculately clean kitchen—one that smelled faintly of ginger. It was yellow. Plants sat on top of all of the cabinets, giving it a warm, forest-y feel. A couple of bubbling pots sat on the stove. Mrs. Li sat me down at the wooden kitchen table. "Let me pour you some tea," she said.

I sat up, about to object, but she'd already turned her back on me, fussing with the electric teakettle.

I took a moment to study the kitchen. At first glance, it was no different from any other kitchen, but small details started to jump out at me. There were a few personal touches here and there: dragon-trimmed dishware, red lanterns hanging from the ceiling, a jade dragon standing guard on the counter over a leather-bound book with Chinese characters stamped on the cover in gold. Turning my head slightly to one side, I saw that the book was a photo album, like you would find in any other house.

Nice. But nothing superlative.

Captain Superlative's mother had a cup of tea, a bowl of chunks of fruit with toothpicks stuck in them, and a plate of almond cookies down in front of me before she finally sat in the chair across the table. Maybe it was just my imagination, but I felt like she was stalling. She ran her fingers over her skirt, smoothing it against her thighs. I noticed that her hands were unsteady.

"Thank you," I said, looking down at the tea.

"Would you like different cookies? I have some Oreos in the pantry."

"No, thanks."

"Chocolate chip?"

"I'm all right."

I wasn't all right.

She nodded slightly and sat there, watching me. Feeling entirely too exposed, I picked up the cup and took a small sip. I didn't like tea, but I managed to swallow it down, scalding my tongue a little. I gave her a smile and she seemed somewhat reassured. "It's very good."

"Good."

An awkward silence followed, before I exhaled through my nose. "I'd like to see . . . Caitlyn."

"She is upstairs. Recovering. Have a cookie."

"Recovering from what?"

"The treatment."

"I don't understand."

Mrs. Li took off her glasses, carefully folding them up and setting them down on the table. She clutched her hands in a formal sort of way. I felt myself bracing for some kind of collision. "Caitlyn is sick."

"Sick."

And I immediately knew. Maybe not in the part of my mind that did the thinking. That part was probably trying very hard not to understand, to protect me. It was more in the part of me that remembered the way my dad used to say the word when he was talking about my mother:

*Sick.*

The weight hanging in the middle. Like the vowel sound was stuck on a piece of gum, gluing the word in the air.

*Your mother is sick.*

She wasn't talking about the flu.

Heat started to well up in my eyes and I found myself gripping my necklace again, so tight that it drove the sharp points of the star into my palm. Why did people do that? Why did they talk around unpleasant things with everyday words like *sick* that could mean anything? I could never really figure it out. Not when I was nine and just starting to understand things. Not now either.

Life, I guess, was easier when you could say the bad thing without actually saying the bad thing.

I realized that I had been silent for . . . a minute? An hour? A year? Captain Superlative's mother sat there patiently, waiting for me. "I'm sorry," I said in a mumble. "Sick?"

"Caitlyn has JMML."

"What?"

"Juvenile myelomonocytic leukemia."

Leukemia. It was a word I knew like my own name. A word that had taken my mother away from me. I'm not sure which was harder, Mrs. Li having to say it or me having to hear it. It didn't matter. It wasn't a competition. "Cancer," I said in a voice that was barely above a whisper.

"Yes."

The hospital. The monster that gobbled up people and never let them go. She hadn't been there trying to help other people. She'd been there for herself. For *herself*. For medicine. For chemicals being pumped into her system. For treatments.

Treatments that were leading to bad seconds and bad days and bad weeks. "She didn't tell me." The words came out sharp.

"I do not think she wanted anyone to know."

"I want to see her."

Mrs. Li shook her head. "She needs to rest."

"I want to see her."

She opened her mouth. And then closed it. Hard. I should have cared more that I was being rude. But a frantic energy was taking hold of me. The kind that could turn into almost anything.

"Wait here," she said, standing up. "I will go see if she is awake."

Captain Superlative's mother slipped out of the room. Her slippered feet padded up the stairs, going around a corner. The floorboards above me creaked with age. There weren't any voices, though.

I leaned over and grabbed the photo album, setting it down on the table and opening it up. Perfectly normal, perfectly happy faces smiled back at me. A husband and a wife and their lovely daughter, Caitlyn, looking just like her picture in the yearbook with that glossy curtain of black hair. They were posing in front of the Museum of Science and Industry. They were lined up along the railing of Wrigley Field. They were standing in front of Deerwood Park Elementary School, sending little Caitlyn off on her first day of classes. No capes or masks or wigs. There was nothing to hide then. They vanished into the woodwork of normal.

Like people were supposed to.

The floorboards creaked again, and I snapped the photo

album shut, sliding it back into place. The unseeing eyes of the jade dragon were the only witness to my crime. Her mother appeared two seconds later, working her hands against each other. "She says you can come up. For a little while. Just take the stairs. First door on the left, once you get to the landing. Go ahead in."

I stood up, mumbling my thanks like I was supposed to. I followed the line of her hand as she gestured around the corner, taking the steps one at a time, my hand sliding along the wooden banister. The numbness was beginning to unravel at the edges, fraying into deep anxiety.

Agitation.

Aggression.

Anger.

# 17

**Captain Superlative's bedroom, at** least, lived up to expectations. In a way. It was a clash between normal and a freak show. The neon-green curtains hung beside bland beige wallpaper with a pattern of cabbage roses. Scattered across the plain white ceiling were glow-in-the-dark stars, stuck on with putty that oozed out between the points. They were arranged in constellations I didn't recognize, telling stories that I didn't know.

On the walls were posters. Larger-than-life superheroes stood with their hands on their hips, their chests open and exposed, their chins raised in defiance. Their bright colors were at odds with the cabbage roses, as if defying them. Beneath the posters, dozens upon dozens of comic books littered the floors, intermingling with valentines and homemade posters for Dagmar's Valentine's Day dance queen campaign. They were ones I hadn't seen. And they were in Captain Superlative's handwriting.

Her bed had a neat little dust ruffle—snow white—peeking out from underneath a tie-dyed comforter that was an explosion of pink and yellow and blue. She was sitting up against half a dozen mismatched pillows on her sturdy, solid headboard, wearing bright pink pj's that were absolutely hanging off of her frail, tiny frame. Her wig was lopsided, like she'd just put it on very quickly. And for once, she wasn't wearing her mask.

Outside of the yearbook pictures and the photo album, it was the first time I'd seen Caitlyn Li's face. She didn't exactly look like the pictures. Her face was gaunt, the lines of her cheeks curving inward slightly, giving her cheekbones an angular quality. Her face was colorless and dull, except for the dark purple bags under her eyes that were painful to look at. The only thing that was the same was the smile, which shone just as brightly as in the photos, as in the halls, from underneath the frayed edge of her mask. She was happy to see me. *Happy.*

It made me want to explode.

"Did you help a lot of citizens in school today?" she asked without any preamble. "I hope you were manning the doors."

"Why didn't you tell me?" My voice came out fierce and sharp, and I didn't even care.

There was no way to hide her expression from me now. Her smile faltered and the lines around her eyes hardened. The tone hit her. Almost like a slap to the face, which made me disgustingly happy. "Tell you what?" Her voice was wary. As well it should have been.

"You *know* what."

I half expected her to squirm and claim she had no idea. People did that sometimes. It was to be expected. But what she said was even more infuriating. "It just didn't come up." She turned decisively to her nightstand, ramping up the speed of a small electric fan that had been whirling with all the urgency of a mini-golf windmill.

Didn't come up? Didn't *come up*? We weren't talking about the weather or the color of her socks! "That's the worst excuse I've ever heard."

"It's not an excuse." She made a big show out of fluffing one of her pillows as the wind blew in her face. It was pale pink with a gray-and-white skunk embroidered across the middle, framed with a thin line of white lace. "You never asked me if I was sick."

"That's not the sort of thing you're supposed to ask."

She shrugged. "It's not the sort of thing that I want to talk about. I've been talking about it my *whole life*." She gave an exasperated sigh. "It started when I was two. I thought it was over and done with, but it's not. It's just not." She wrinkled her nose, sinking back. "It's never over."

"You should have told me!" I made a futile, useless gesture, as though I wanted to hit something. But there was nothing to hit.

"Well, I'm sorry."

"Sorry? You're *sorry*?"

"Yes." She looked me dead in the eyes. "Sorry."

Did she think she *actually* had superpowers? Did she believe that a magic word was going to sweep away the things she wanted to disappear? I shook my head. Magic wasn't real. "It's not that easy."

"Why not?"

"Because!" How could she not understand something like that? "Because it's not!"

"Life doesn't always have to be so complicated, Janey."

"It's life!" Complicated seemed like as good a definition of life as any I'd ever heard.

"Well, why do you think I wanted to become a superhero?"

The question came out of nowhere. "What?"

She brightened a little bit, in that way of hers. "There's nothing complicated about that. It feels right." She shrugged. "It's easy."

"Easy?"

"You just have to do the right thing. You don't have to worry about what people think. You don't have to dress like other people dress. You don't have to be afraid of anything." I saw a change come over her, one I hadn't anticipated. The brightness faded. Before, I'd seen her without any cloth over her face. But now—now I was finally seeing Caitlyn Li without a mask. "Superheroes are more themselves than anyone else. They're strong. Smart. Capable. Superheroes are never scared of the dark."

"So that's the reason." I was back in the library, back in that day that we never seemed to talk about, holding the yearbook in my lap, wondering why anyone would suddenly decide to become a superhero. I'd never come up with a real answer, but even in guessing, I would never have imagined this. I couldn't have. It was just too strange and horrible. "That's the real reason."

"What?"

"That's why you wanted to do this whole superhero thing. It wasn't about doing good. It was about being . . ." I struggled to find the right word. "Selfish. You're being selfish!"

Caitlyn sat up in bed. "What?"

"Yeah!" There was no turning back. "Yeah! That's exactly it!" I kicked one of the comic books on the floor, glaring at it. This was the source of the infection, what had driven her insane. I suddenly wanted to rip all of them to pieces.

"What are you talking about?"

"You were doing it for you! Because superheroes are never afraid!" It made so much sense to me that I barely even heard her. I'd solved my puzzle. I just didn't like the answer.

"Janey! That's not the reason!"

"And you are. You're afraid. Don't lie!"

"Well, of *course* I'm afraid!"

It should have felt like a victory. It was. I'd been right. But I felt a hollowness settle over the room instead. Caitlyn couldn't look at me. She fidgeted, reaching under her comforter and pulling out a red sheet. Her cape, I realized, seeing the big *C* glued to the back. She held it against her shoulder like a security blanket. Which was what it had been, all along.

A lucky red security blanket.

"I don't want to die," she said quietly. "My parents had plans for me. *I* had plans for me. But I'm going to. We thought it was gone, but it's not. It's here, and it's here to stay, and I'm going to die. We all are, eventually. But a little bit sooner for me." Her voice got bigger again. "I don't want to go without actually being someone first. I don't want to go quietly."

"That's what people do," I said.

Caitlyn shook her head. "You can't tell me how to die any more than you can tell me how to live."

It sounded too much like a riddle. Like something a comic-book character would say. "This isn't how people face death!" I kicked another one of the comic books. I wanted to reach out and shake her. I wanted to drag her down to the photo album and show her all of those pictures, remind her that she was normal.

"How would you know?"

"Because I've seen it!"

She frowned. "Your mother?"

It was a part of me I didn't want to share. Least of all with her, least of all with someone I didn't feel like I could trust. "Don't talk about her." Not a request, but a demand.

"I'm not the same person as her."

"Yeah. I know that. At least when she left me, it was honest."

"Janey!"

I wasn't with Caitlyn then. I was nine years old again, trying to understand what my life was without my mother. Nothing felt right. As if I had to relearn how to do everything, to compensate for that lost presence.

*She's gone.*

It was happening again. Captain Superlative would leave another void. I suddenly saw my life without her. I got a taste of it this afternoon, after all. Hadn't I? Tyler and his friends. They were laughing. At *me*. Of *course*. Why hadn't I realized it sooner? Everyone would laugh at me. The freak. The only freak. Once she was gone, that was all I would be. Facing down those doors by myself.

And it was all her fault. It was the sick, twisted legacy she'd cursed me with, without my realizing it. The isolation I'd once feared from my mother's death was going to be Caitlyn Li's doing instead.

When she left me.

"Janey?"

I'd lost track of time, lost track of my own silence. It was rude, but I didn't care. I'd been rude plenty today. "Forget it." I shook my head, feeling like it was underwater. "Just forget all of it."

"Janey, please." She leaned forward, holding her hand out to me. "I don't understand. Why are you so angry?"

I stared down at her hand, overcome by the fact that it wouldn't be there for me forever. I would have to walk down the halls of Deerwood Park Middle School without her warmth behind my shoulder. Alone. And different. And *that*—that was forever. "I have to go," I said, stepping away from her and out of reach.

"Don't leave." She tried to stretch forward, to grab me, but I was too far away and she began coughing.

"See you around," I said, turning from her. I paused before taking a step, adding, "Caitlyn."

"Captain"—she wheezed and coughed and struggled to get it out—"Superlative."

I whirled around, balling up my hands into fists at my sides. "Your name is Caitlyn!"

She got the coughing under control. And much to my surprise, she nodded. Just barely. "My name is Caitlyn. But Captain Superlative is who I am."

There was a difference. Even in my rage, I could see the difference. I just didn't want to admit it. I didn't want her to be right. How dare she make me stick my neck out into danger like that? How dare she hide the truth? She didn't *deserve* to be right, not about anything.

So I stared. A stone-cold, dead stare.

Caitlyn leaned back against her pillows, looking incredibly serene, if not a little pink in the face. "Who are you, Janey?" she asked me.

I couldn't take another second of it.

I stomped out of the room. I heard her calling after me, but I didn't answer and I didn't look back. I took the stairs two at a time, tearing back through the kitchen and the entry hall. I forgot my shoes and threw the door open, letting myself out, cutting across the crisp, silvery lawn and up the sidewalk. Salt crunched under my wet socks, my breath coming out in bright white bursts of fog. The hot tears that had started building up in the Li house fell down the sides of my face, blurring my vision so I couldn't see where I was going.

But somehow I kept going all the way. On instinct.

The next thing I knew, I was curled up and sobbing on a cold bench, across the street from the hospital. Betty Grossman's bench. A loving daughter, sister, wife, and mother.

Just like my mother.

I cried with my whole body, shoulders heaving, stomach tightening. And for all the drama and heat and noise, if anyone had stopped to ask me why I was sobbing, I wouldn't have been able to put it into words. It was so many things, but above all else, I was in mourning for what I saw as the end of my life. Not my *life* life, but my social existence at Deerwood Park Middle School. I hadn't even realized it was over until I pictured myself standing at those doors by myself. I had been alone before. Alone and invisible. But things were different now.

I hated different.

Defective.

Deranged.

Doomed.

# 18

**I walked home after dark—the foggy** night obscured the stars—went right to my room, and collapsed face-first on the bed. I breathed in the familiar scent of my comforter (fabric softener and ice cream, I think) and fell asleep. In a hazy, distant sort of way, I was aware of my dad coming in and taking off my wet socks, covering up my feet with a warm pillow. He asked me if I wanted dinner. I said no. And then I drifted back to sleep again.

When I woke up, Selina was curled up in a ball, nestled in the bend of my legs. I raised my head slightly, the bleary red numbers of my digital clock reading 9:14. Too late to get up and do anything. Too early to go back to sleep. I heard the springs of my bed creak and felt the weight of my dad sitting down beside me. He sat still, letting me grow accustomed to his presence. And then, after some time, he put his hand on my head and started stroking my hair.

It felt safe. Like when I was younger. Like when I woke up from the nightmares of monsters and hospitals.

"Rough day?" Dad asked.

"You could say that," I said, turning my face back into the covers so that my voice was muffled in my sheets.

"Do you want to talk about it?"

"No."

He continued to stroke my hair. "Are you lying?"

I frowned a little bit, my dry lips catching against the covers. "Yes," I finally said.

He didn't scold me. Or ask why. Or even make a joke. He just sat there. "I'll wait."

And he waited.

I finally turned my head, glancing up at him. He looked hazy and white, a spirit from beyond, protecting me. Except that he couldn't. He could never protect me. As warm and as safe as I felt, eventually I would have to go back to school. "It was all just some kind of stupid game," I said.

"What was?"

As if he didn't already know. It had been consuming my life—our lives—for over a month. "Captain Superlative," I said. "Because she was afraid. Because she didn't want to live in her reality."

"Do you always want to live in yours?" he asked, predictably enough. "People always want to escape their realities. That's why we have books and music and theatre and monster-truck rallies."

"This was very, very different."

"Why?"

"Because this is how she's dealing with *dying*."

Dying. What a word. Saying it out loud was violent and rough. Worse than Dagmar saying *freak*. The *D*-sound at the beginning was a stab wound in the air. My dad felt it, I could tell. His hand slowed on my head for a moment, hovering there. "Dying." He said it softer, but the sound was still the same.

"Leukemia."

There was another unpleasant word.

"Juvenile something-something leukemia. A relapse."

His palm fell on the crown of my head, cradling it the same way that he cradled Selina when she was a newborn kitten left on the doorstep to his office. "Oh, Janey." I almost didn't hear him; he was so, so very quiet. "I'm so sorry to hear that, sweetheart."

*She's gone.*

I felt him try to pull me up against him. He wanted to hug me. But I resisted. Hugs were for sadness. I didn't want to be *sad*. It was easier to be angry. I turned over onto my other side, facing away from him and disrupting Selina's sleep. Directly in front of me was the wooden headboard of my bed, the same one I'd had in our old house. It had been my mother's when she was my age.

Cancer sucked.

I laughed a little. It was a dry, mirthless laugh. Rusty, like I hadn't used it in a while. "Guess I know what the big *C* stands for," I said.

"Do you?"

"That's what they call cancer, isn't it? 'The Big *C*.'" It

had been staring me in the face the whole time, I just hadn't seen it.

"Sometimes."

Lightly, I ran my fingers over the grooves in the headboard. I knew each scratch and scar by heart. My favorite was a little star-shaped one near the top. I traced the shape of it with my index finger. I wondered if my mother had ever done the same thing. What had she been thinking about when she was my age? What hopes and dreams had she had? Hopes and dreams that would never be realized, because the Big C would take her away too early, too soon. It wasn't fair. But at least she hadn't started running around in a cape and tights. "It's not the way it was with Mom," I said. "I remember."

"Janey, there's no one way to do things. I wish you understood that. People are different. People are *supposed* to be different."

"Right. Or we'd all be named Bob."

"Exactly. There are no fewer than ten hundred thousand million different ways to be human. Bob is just one of them."

"I'd take that right now. I'd be Bob in a heartbeat if I could."

"Why?"

I let out an exasperated, frustrated noise. "I got dragged into the middle of someone else's story." And now I was stuck there. It was a strange and mysterious sea and my life raft was dissolving like salt.

"You tried something new. It was scary and exciting and beyond your experiences, but you jumped right into that abyss where the future lives."

"I shouldn't have."

Dad put a hand on my shoulder and, for a moment, I wanted to cling to him. "You were enjoying your adventures."

"I put my neck on the line. All because of some stupid lie." I rolled back over to face him, feeling the heaviness of my eyes, still swollen from crying. Selina mewed, hopped down from the bed, and slipped under it. I swear she gave me a dirty look. A very familiar sort of green-eyed look. "Dagmar Hagen hates me."

"So?" Dad asked. I knew he wouldn't understand, of course. How could he? "So what?"

"So," I said, "soon Captain Superlative will be gone, and so will the lie. And then what? What am I supposed to do, Dad? I have a reputation as a freak's assistant now."

He slipped his fingers under my chin, tilting it slightly to look me in the eyes. "At least you're someone, Janey."

Now he was speaking in riddles too. I pulled out of his reach and slid off the bed. I stalked to the little desk against the wall, near the foot of the bed. Right there in the middle of stacks of drawings and lists of potential good deeds was my social-studies test, with the big red 100 percent circled on the top. Below the grade was the first question. About ostracism, of course.

Oddball.

Outlander.

Outsider.

Outcast.

"Great," I said. "I'm *someone*. Someone I'm not supposed to be." Someone who was dangerous to the state. Someone who would be ostracized.

"How do you know?"

"I just know!"

"Janey, that's ridiculous. You have absolutely no proof that this isn't exactly who you're supposed to be."

"It's not who I want to be."

"I know, Bob. I know."

I glared down at the test. "What do I do?"

"I wish I could give you a simple answer, Janey." He laughed softly. "It would make my job a lot easier."

"I want things to go back to the way they were. Before Captain Superlative. Caitlyn. Whatever."

"You don't mean that."

"Yes. I do."

He was quiet. Too quiet. It made my skin crawl a little bit. And it wasn't much better when he finally spoke. "So what do you do?"

"Tomorrow," I said, "everything goes back to normal. The way it was. The way it's supposed to be."

"Well..."

The *well* trailed off into infinity.

"Well what?"

"If that's what you want."

I turned around, the surprise written all across my face. "That's it? Just like that?"

"Did you want more of a fight?"

"No. But I was expecting one."

He stood up, the bed groaning. "Sometimes, Janey, being a parent means letting your children make the mistakes that they might need to make."

"What does that mean?"

"It means I know my daughter." He came over to my side, kissing my head. "Probably better than she knows herself right now. And I know that Jane Esther Silverman is going to make the right choices. Eventually."

And he left.

The right choice was to go back. I'd been Plain Jane for a very long time. Nothing but air drifting through Deerwood Park Middle School. I could be her again. I wanted to be her again. I needed to be her again.

What was the alternative?

My social-studies test taunted me. At least in ancient Greece, when people were ostracized, they left the city. It wouldn't be so easy for me. I would be thrown out and still be forced to see the very people who had ostracized me. Day after day after day. Plain Jane was my only hope.

I knocked the test off the desk, sending it fluttering to the ground. Underneath was a stray heart, one of the valentines that Caitlyn and I had cut out. I'd kept it, thinking that I'd make a secret one for *her.* I picked it up, turning it over in my fingers. And then, overcome with anger, I crumpled it up into a tight and untidy wad in my hand and threw it against the wall.

The next morning, I woke up to the alarm at six. Normally, Captain . . . Caitlyn . . . and I met at 6:45 by the front doors, to open them for the teachers who arrived with boxes of supplies and piles of papers.

I hit the snooze button.

At 6:55, I got up and got dressed in jeans and a plain white sweatshirt. Hair loose. My mother's necklace. Blue Shoes.

My reflection in the mirror was appropriately ordinary. I could have been anyone.

"Good morning, Bob," my dad said to me as he pulled out a carton of orange juice from the fridge.

"Good morning."

We didn't talk about anything except the German shepherd he was seeing later today. There was something on the tip of his tongue, but he didn't say it.

I wondered why.

I wondered if it had something to do with those "mistakes I needed to make" or whatever. But I was sure that I was doing the right thing, that I wasn't making a mistake.

And I was wrong.

# 19

**I'd forgotten the way Dagmar's voice** sounded when she zeroed in on someone. Sugary-sweet, almost flirtatious. A little too coy. For weeks, she hadn't dared. Not with Paige, not with anyone. The looming threat of Caitlyn's presence had been a powerful one. Or maybe just the looming threat of another dramatic exit. But for the past four days, no one had seen any sign of a red cape.

Except for me.

The ticking time bomb was itching to go off.

We were sitting in first-period Language Arts, but Mr. Collins was down in the office, copying a short story for homework. A cluster of girls hovered around Dagmar's phone (a new one her mother had just gotten her as a "just because" present), watching a movie trailer. Everyone else was talking.

Everyone except me. I sat alone in the back of the classroom, counting the motes of dust. Except I kept losing count.

One of the soccer players came into the classroom, carrying a basket full of bright pink flowers. To raise funds for the team, they'd been selling them all week. An idea Dagmar had stolen from Kohn last year. For a dollar, you could have a flower and a chocolate heart delivered to one of your classmates. Dagmar glanced up at her and said, "Oh, hi, Meredith," in that oozy tone of voice of hers, and I cringed.

"Hey, Dagmar."

With a wave of her hand, Dagmar shooed away the moths around her, thumbing off the video. "Got a delivery?"

"Yeah," Meredith said, crossing the room over to Tyler. "This one is for you," she said, handing him a flower with a heart-shaped card and a piece of candy tied to the stem with a pink ribbon.

Tyler took it, flipping the card over to read the signature. His face split into a grin and then he turned to look at me, of all people. "Hey, thanks so much, Janey!" he said with a wave.

Beside him, Kevin gave him a nudge. "Nice, Romeo."

Tyler swatted him away.

I felt my face go white-hot. I hadn't sent a flower to Tyler.

Or anyone else, for that matter.

Caitlyn and I were supposed to start delivering our valentines today. But she was home sick and they were probably sitting in a box on the floor of her room somewhere. Forgotten.

"Oh. Hey. Here's another one for you," Meredith said, handing a second flower to Tyler.

"Way to go, Gaston," one of his other friends teased.

He glanced at the signature. This time his grin looked a little uncomfortable to me. "Thanks again, Janey."

Two cards in my name?

But it was only getting worse. Meredith produced a third, and a fourth, and a fifth flower in rapid succession, everyone watching as Tyler read my name each time and the pile of pink petals grew on his desk. Giggles and whispers broke out across the room. "Hey, all celebrities have stalkers," Kevin said.

Eyes bore down on me. Dagmar, who I realized had lifted her phone to film the whole thing, asked in her most innocent voice, "Five flowers, Jane? Don't you think that's just a little bit desperate?"

More giggles. Meredith looked like she was having the time of her life. "No," I said desperately, feeling a pulse in my cheeks. "I didn't send them. It wasn't me."

"We get the point, Jane," Dagmar continued, enjoying every syllable. "You have a crush on Tyler."

She panned the camera over to me.

I knew without a doubt who had sent the flowers.

Mercifully, there weren't any more flowers that morning. Maybe that was just because I didn't have any more classes with Tyler until after lunch. But I could feel everyone watching me everywhere I went. Every laugh in the hallway, somehow I knew was related to me. What else could there possibly be to laugh about?

I needed to get away.

At lunch, I decided I would eat in the bathroom. If I could just stay out of sight for a while, everyone would forget the whole thing. I was foolish enough to believe in my plan. Get into the cafeteria. Get lunch. Disappear without ever touching lava. Everything would be fine.

It would have been nice.

Paige was waiting for me outside of the double doors to the cafeteria. "Janey," she said, trying to flag me down.

I shook my head, trying to push past her. "Can't talk right now."

"No, listen." She grabbed my arm. "There's something you need to know."

"I'll catch you later," I said, pulling away from her.

"Janey!"

I knew I should have stopped to listen to Paige the second I walked into the cafeteria. Something was up. For one thing, it was way too quiet. There were a few whispered conversations here and there, but not the whirlwind of chatter that everyone was used to. And as I walked in, it got even quieter. Except for one shrill, uncontrolled giggle that rose up out of a corner. I turned to follow the sound, but a splash of color drew my attention away.

Plastered up against the wall were posters. Dozens and dozens of posters covered with pictures of my face. Someone had taken a picture of me. It wasn't flattering. One eye was squinty and my mouth was open, like I was just about to take a bite out of something. The horrible thing was blown up, copied dozens of times and shining with glitter and sequins and cutouts of tiaras, surrounded by pink and red hearts.

CITIZENS!
Vote for Jane Silverman
for Seventh-Grade
Valentine's Day Queen.

The slogan repeated over and over and over again in gloriously ugly Comic Sans MS. And to make matters even worse, half of the posters had phrases like "Kohn Junior High for Jane" and "Kohn Supports Jane Silverman." The other half had pictures of Tyler on them, wearing the fake plastic crown.

They were awful. Garish and gaudy and ridiculous and nothing at all like me. They looked like desperation splashed on a wall. And as I stared up at them, mortified, the laughter began to swell. Giggles from the cheerleaders and hoots and hollers from the jocks and every other shade of laughter in between.

"We get it," I heard Dagmar say from somewhere in the middle of it all. "Hashtag-cryforattention." She was snapping pictures of the whole scene with her phone. "Why don't you just put on a cape or something?"

I turned to look at her, but found Tyler, who had just walked in with his friends. They all burst into roaring laughs, slapping him on the shoulders. Tyler rubbed the back of his neck, averting his gaze and looking embarrassed.

Nothing ever embarrassed Tyler Jeffries.

Ever.

Not until today.

"I didn't..." I tried to explain, but the words stuck in my throat.

"Not a bad idea," Kevin said. He turned to face the back of the room. "Janey for queen!"

From somewhere behind me, a chant started. "Janey! Janey! Janey!"

"No!" I spun in a circle, their faces blurring together.

"Janey! Janey! Janey!"

"I didn't . . . I never!"

"Janey! Janey! Janey!"

It got louder. They wouldn't let up. Mocking me was apparently too much to resist. I felt like I was going to be sick. I was drowning in my own name, my eyes filling up with tears. I wrapped my arms around my stomach, raced past Tyler and out of the cafeteria, ripped into the bathroom, and locked the door behind me.

No lock could stop the shameful, taunting chant from echoing in my brain.

*Janey! Janey! Janey!*

The rest of the school day was impossible. I drifted through it in a dreamlike state, not allowing myself to meet anyone's eyes. I just wanted to go home. To escape. And when the final bell rang, I was out of my seat like a rocket, racing to the library. I would return my books and sneak out of one of the side exits.

And hopefully disappear.

But, of course, the day couldn't make anything easy for me. Because there was Dagmar, lingering near the library door, grinning in that horrible, predatory way of hers. "You learned your lesson yet, freak?" she asked, brushing her ponytail back off her shoulder.

At least she'd dispensed with all the fake sweetness.

I tried to slip past her into the library, but she blocked the way like she had for Paige, planting a hand on the wall with a loud thunk. Too high for me to step over, too low for me to duck under. I took a step to go around her other side, but the hallway was bustling and kids went by, blocking the path. No choice but to wait.

I stared down at my Blue Shoes.

"Have you figured out that it isn't Halloween?"

"Dagmar..."

Her face came dangerously close to mine. "If you mess with me again, you're going to wish I'd only sent flowers and made a few lousy posters."

"Fine," I said hotly. "I get it. I won't bother you."

"And what about your freak friend?"

"She's not my friend."

"Oh. Well. I guess freaks can't really have friends, can they?"

I saw Kevin passing by, unsteady on his crutches. He caught my eyes for a second, but then he saw Dagmar. Looking panicked and afraid, he quickly turned away, hobbling off as fast as he could. Coming from the other direction was Meredith Li. I raised a hand to try to flag her down, but she spotted Dagmar and immediately pulled a compact out of her purse, breezing by and pretending to check her lipstick.

It kept going like that. Everyone scurried away in fear of Queen Dagmar Hagen.

She was *back*.

It occurred to me in that minute that I knew the name of every single person who passed: Sixth graders, seventh graders, eighth graders. Kids on the quiz bowl team. Kids in the school play. Black kids. White kids. Asian kids. Smart kids. Jocks, cheerleaders, and mathletes. Popular kids. Outsiders. Only children and new kids. Classmates since kindergarten.

Each of them paused for a second, lips parting slightly. But then each of them saw Dagmar and changed their mind. They wanted to help me. I could see it in their eyes. They wanted to reach out for me, to protect me.

But not one would dare throw themselves between Dagmar and her prey. That had been something only one person was willing to do.

The frightened gazes didn't escape Dagmar's attention. Her lips curled up. She was loving every second of it. "You don't have friends, Jane."

"Stop." I barely said it. I doubt she heard it.

It wouldn't have made a difference.

"You know what you are, Jane? *Nothing.*"

"I..."

"I feel sorry for you. I really do. Not pretty. Not special. Not popular. *You're*"—she made an absent, futile gesture—"*nothing.*" And she laughed. It was the worst sound I'd ever heard. "I don't know how you can stand being alive and being nothing. I'd just want to curl up and die." She took a step closer to me. I could feel waves of heat radiating off of her skin. "Don't you? Just want to curl up? And die?"

What could I do but tell her the truth? "Yes," I said.

"Could you be more tragic?"

"Dagmar."

"More pathetic?"

"Please."

I felt her move more than I actually saw it. Heat whistled through the air and I looked up to see her draw her hand back, palm open. I clenched my jaw in anticipation of the blow.

"Dagmar!"

We both turned to look at the same time, to see who would dare challenge her.

It was Tyler. He marched over to where we were standing, grabbing Dagmar by the wrist. "What are you doing?"

I expected her to adopt her customary sweetness. To bat her pretty eyes at Tyler and flirt. But apparently, that ship had sailed. She twisted her wrist out of his grasp and glared straight at me again. "Oh, *nothing*."

With that, she was gone. She blazed away from the library with a flip of her hair, as if what had happened had truly been nothing.

But it hadn't been. In the silence between each pulse of my heart, I could hear myself breaking. I stared down at the ground, my cheeks flushed and hot. And I wondered how I was supposed to go on with life after all of that.

Tyler looked at me. "You all right, Janey?"

"What's wrong, Janey?" It was a pair of sixth graders I'd helped with language arts last week looking over at me.

"Janey?" It was an eighth grader I'd given a mint to, once upon a time. "You look like you're about to cry."

"Are you okay, Janey?" April. Dagmar Hagen's right-hand woman.

More voices joined the chorus. More kids began to stop and slow and look at me, faces filled with concern.

"Janey?"

"Janey?"

"Janey?"

It reminded me of the chanting from the cafeteria. The mock praise. The laughter at my expense. I couldn't hear their words, their concern. All I heard was my name, over and over and over again. And it was all too much.

I took off down the hall, careening past every door until I found the girls' bathroom. I threw myself in just as the dam inside me broke. My legs gave out from under me and I hit the grungy tiles, crumpling up with a few breathy sobs.

And I cried.

I cried harder than I knew I was capable of crying.

Everything felt like it was coming out of me, every last drop of anguish and sadness and pain. I cried my guts out. I cried past the point when I knew that my tears had dried up.

I don't know how long I sat there on the floor. But at some point, a pair of old, muddy sneakers suddenly appeared and filled my vision. "Janey?" Paige. I knew it before I even looked up to see her concerned expression.

I shook my head. "Just go."

Paige sat down on the ground next to me, setting her books—in my old bag—off to one side. Like my dad, she didn't say anything at first. She just sat there, allowing me to feel her beside me.

"There's a bunch of kids standing around out there," she said, jutting her chin in the direction of the door. "They said you were upset."

I nodded miserably.

"Dagmar?" she asked.

"Yeah."

Paige exhaled through her nose. "Let me guess." Her voice got a little deeper and cartoony. "*You're nothing.*" Not a bad impersonation of Dagmar, all things considered. I might have laughed, if I hadn't felt so miserable and so utterly empty.

"Yeah," I said again.

"That's an old Hagen classic," she said in her own voice. "She's been doing it for years."

"I know."

I'd seen it, hadn't I? That day by the lockers, when I'd felt Dagmar cross those lines with Paige. I'd had to brace myself, I was so startled. And then Caitlyn had shown up to save Paige.

While I stood there watching, pretending not to notice.

Like Kevin.

Like Meredith.

Like everyone who had just left me at the mercy of Dagmar.

"I know," I said again, quietly.

"Makes you kind of wish the earth would open up and swallow you whole, doesn't it?"

I sighed. "Yeah."

"There was a pretty good streak going for a while, though," Paige said. "With Captain Superlative—"

"Caitlyn Li."

She went on as if I hadn't interrupted. "There to shut her up."

"Just a freak accident," I said, glaring at my shoes.

"Accident? No. Freak?" She frowned, nodded, and

shrugged. "Maybe a little. I mean, compared to..." She trailed off.

I looked up at her. "Compared to what?"

Paige wetted her lips and scooted back a little to lean against the wall next to me. "For as long as I can remember," she said, "Dagmar's been awful to me."

I sat up. "I know."

"Of course you do. Everyone knows. It's not a secret. Because there's always someone there to see it." She held out her palms. "Someone watching it. Someone letting it happen to me."

We held a look for a moment, before I turned away.

"The hardest part is when people watch and do nothing." Paige looked deeper into my eyes. "Which is most of the time."

"When people just watch?"

"Or look away." She smiled sadly. I could hear it in her voice, even without seeing it. "That's when you really feel like you're *nothing*." She paused. "Someone was watching you today, huh?"

Everyone. Everyone had been watching me. And no one said a word.

"Didn't do anything to stop it?" Paige asked.

"No," I said.

Not at first, anyway.

Tyler tried to stand up for me. Then kids asked if I was okay. But it was all too late. The damage had been done. Dagmar had won.

Paige slapped her palm down on my knee, rocking it from side to side. "Welcome to my world."

We sat in silence for a moment, before it occurred to me that there was something I needed to say. Something that I'd owed Paige. For a long, long time. "I'm sorry, Paige."

She smiled. "Hey, I'm not looking for apologies."

"Still."

"Thanks." She gave my leg a little squeeze. "You look like you could use a friend right now."

"Yeah," I said.

She was quiet a moment, thoughtful. Then she looked down along the line of her shoulder at me. "Come with me. Come to my house."

"What?"

"Let's go. Right now."

"You sure you want to be seen with me?" After all, I was probably going to be the butt of every joke for the rest of time.

"It's cute that you think I would care about something like that." She paused a second. "You got plans for dinner tonight?"

"I don't think so."

"Then you're coming with me."

There was something about the way Paige said it . . . there was a spark of knowing in her eyes that I hadn't seen before. Something she was holding back. Something important that was couched in the invitation. I didn't understand it. But somewhere along the line, I'd discovered that if there was one thing I couldn't stand, it was an unsolved mystery, an unanswered question. I had to know things. Everything. And Paige had something on her mind. I wanted—no, I *needed*—to find out what it was.

# 20

**Answers, unfortunately, are elusive** and temperamental creatures. You have to fight for them. In my case, in order to figure out why Paige wanted me to come over, I would have to run through a gauntlet first.

Paige hadn't been kidding about what was waiting for me outside the bathroom. As the door opened, a group of students—ten, fifteen, twenty maybe—looked up expectantly, like a herd of meerkats. I kept my head ducked low, huddling close to Paige. I knew if I made eye contact I'd feel it all over again. That sense of helplessness, that feeling of being at Dagmar's mercy.

I heard kids calling out to me, though. Tyler and the others. I knew each and every one of them. They'd become a part of the fabric of my existence, through opening the door and handing out mints and offering help in the library. The new fort kid, Nicole. Raquel, the seventh-grade class president. Zach from the yearbook club. Darnell, who was captain of the mathletes. And April, who I'd pushed away, mistaking a third grader's fear for something more sinister.

"Janey?"

"Are you all right, Janey?"

"Forget about her, Janey."

"It'll be okay, Janey."

"Janey."

"Janey."

"Janey."

It was the cafeteria all over again, with the *Janey! Janey! Janey!*

I shuddered, thinking about it.

Paige put her arm around me and led me down the hall. Most of the kids stayed rooted to the spot and watched, falling silent, but Tyler trotted along behind us. "Is she going to be okay?" he asked.

I cringed at the sound of his voice, ducking my head against Paige's shoulder. Go away, I thought. Just go away.

"Yeah," Paige said, sensing my discomfort.

"Just ignore Dagmar, Janey," he said. "And they say *I'm* a drama queen."

*Just go away.*

"It'll be fine," Paige said.

"Okay," he said. And reluctantly, he added: "I have to get to rehearsal."

"Go. I'll take care of her."

"Bye, Paige. Bye, Janey." He started to walk down the hall. I could hear his footsteps retreating, but then they stopped. "You know," he said, "I get it. I know what it's like to be made fun of. Theatre kids get made fun of all the time. *I* get made fun of all the time. You can't take it too seriously." A pause. "So don't. It doesn't matter, Janey. None of it matters."

The German shepherd, as it turned out, was every bit the hassle that my dad anticipated. He was relieved—and pleasantly surprised—when I called to tell him that I had an invitation to dinner. I think he was sure that if I was left to my own devices, I'd eat nachos and Pixy Stix, with ice cream for dessert, and call it a well-balanced meal. Instead, it was roasted chicken, fruit salad, creamed spinach, and the best macaroni and cheese I'd ever tasted.

Paige's family lived in an apartment building not too far from where my dad and I lived. Her mother reminded me of the Betty Grossman I'd always imagined. Plump. Friendly. With gentle hands and a laugh that rippled through her body. Paige's four older sisters were all incredibly beautiful, just like her. And her little brother, Tyrone, was a ball of kinetic energy, bouncing from one thing to the next. I didn't get to meet her dad. He was in the city at an event. But from the pictures on the wall, I could see that he had the same soulful eyes as Paige.

Not a clown. Not a hobo. Not a loser.

Not even a little bit.

After dinner, Paige and I shut ourselves up in the room she shared with one of her sisters, who seemed to be involved in a seriously goopy text conversation with her boyfriend. She ignored us while we sat together on Paige's bed, which was up against the wall, under a poster for the Chicago Symphony Orchestra.

We talked for a while, then Paige produced a box of markers. The next thing I knew, I was drawing a tattoo on her arm. It was a flower—a hibiscus—with delicate, fluttering petals along the back of her hand, and a long, leafy stem that snaked up the length of her arm, wrapping itself around her elbow.

"You ought to join the art club," Paige said, smiling as I started to shade in the petals with a pink marker.

I stared at her hand, the tip of my tongue peeking out of the corner of my mouth as I concentrated. "I'm not that good."

"You don't have to be. It's not like anyone's paying you to do it. It's just for fun." She snorted. "You think my songs for choir are any good?"

"That one you were working on in the cafeteria sounded pretty good," I said. Not that I knew good music from bad. I couldn't explain my feelings well, but my instincts just told me that music was written into Paige's soul.

Paige's lips twisted slightly. "I sang that for you, didn't I?"

"Yeah."

"I forgot about that." Paige paused a moment. "The first song I ever wrote," she told me, jutting her chin in her sister's direction, "was about her last boyfriend. Benny. He was a junior and he was in love with his car."

I grinned, popping the cap on the pink marker and reaching for the red. "You're kidding me."

Paige shook her head. "Dead serious. And it was an *ugly* car. An '82 Citroën BX."

I didn't know anything about cars, but from the way Paige said it, it had to be pretty hideous. "Oh yeah?"

"Yup."

"How'd the song go?"

She closed her eyes, humming for a second before she broke into a pretty little tune that reminded me of birdsong:

*And he told me he loved her,*
*I thought it was weird.*
*She didn't have a rear bumper.*
*She only went in second gear.*

*But when he said her name*
*His eyes lit up like stars.*
*So how could I complain?*
*My sister's boyfriend loves a car!*

The two of us lit up. Paige's sister shot us more than a few dirty looks, but that only made it feel funnier somehow.

"I wish I had sisters," I said when I finally calmed down enough to wipe the tears away from my eyes.

Paige wrinkled her nose. "If you had four, you'd think differently. Try waiting for hours just to get into the bathroom. I think there's some kind of weird rule that says once you start high school, you need to spend at least five hours a day in there."

I laughed, uncapping the red marker to shade the inner parts of the hibiscus petals. "Maybe."

"I'm just glad they're all in high school. Wouldn't want them anywhere near me during the school day."

"Yeah?"

"Yeah." Paige paused. And that same knowing look from before returned to her eyes. "Dagmar's an only child too," she said. She jerked her thumb over one shoulder, toward the wall. "Her family lives in the apartment next to ours."

"I didn't know that." Somehow, I'd gotten it into my mind that surely Dagmar lived in a mansion. With glass elevators and gold-plated toothbrushes. And a moat. Filled with alligators.

She nodded. "Her mom and mine used to be real good friends when I was little."

"Used to be?"

"Paige!" Little Tyrone appeared in the doorway, barreling into the room and jumping up on the bed behind Paige. Quickly, I lifted the marker, pointing the tip up so I wouldn't smear the flower. Tyrone had an orange plastic dinosaur toy in one fist and a Ping-Pong paddle in the other. "The demon is coming. He's going to attack the fort. Get ready!"

I grinned, remembering my own games of make-believe, hunting after demons and dragons and such. Sometimes, April and I would throw sheets over our heads and grab butterfly nets, going hunting for aliens in the basement. But Paige got serious, drawing Tyrone's arms over her shoulders from behind and giving him a gentle hug. "You know what I think?" she said, leaning her head back to look up at her little brother.

"What?"

"I think you should go ask Mom if you can watch cartoons."

He let out an indignant huff. "But I *already* watched cartoons."

"You tell her I said it was all right."

Tyrone debated it for a moment, but then nodded. "Okay." And with that, he hopped off of her bed, racing out of the room and making strange airplane sounds.

"He's so cute," I said.

Paige sighed, looking out the door after him. "Yeah," she said, pressing her lips together.

"What's wrong?"

Paige didn't answer. As it turned out, she didn't have to. The answer spoke for itself.

From the other side of Paige's wall, I heard a door open then slam shut. There was a voice. Deep and scratchy. Like the bellow of a furnace. "Look at this place! Dagmar!" it roared. "Get in here right now!"

"Here we go again," Paige's sister said.

"Don't you talk to her that way!" a second voice shouted back, this one high and shrieky.

Wide-eyed, I looked from the wall to Paige to the sister and back to Paige again. "Who's that?" I asked.

"Dagmar's parents," Paige said.

Paige's sister rolled her eyes. "The demon's attacking the fort. *Again.*" She stuck in her earbuds and turned up her music so loud that I could hear it across the room.

I heard a third voice on the other side of the wall. One that I knew. Dagmar. "Hi, Daddy. I was going to clean it up. I just got back from practice."

It was funny. Not funny ha-ha. Funny strange. I knew it was Dagmar. I recognized the sound of her voice, the pitch and the tone. But at the same time, it was like I was hearing an entirely different person. The person I was hearing was meek. Was small.

Was afraid.

The Dagmar Hagen I knew inspired fear, she didn't feel it.

No. The voice was un-Dagmar.

Her father roared again. "There's mud all over the place!" There was something wrong about the way his words came out. They were slurred and erratic.

"I'll get the carpet cleaner," the un-Dagmar said. "Right now."

"You bet you will. You and your useless soccer shoes."

"Are you listening to me? I said, don't talk to her that way!" Dagmar's mother said.

"Shut up!" her father replied. "I'll deal with you later."

"Oh, you will, will you? You'll 'deal' with me?"

The un-Dagmar's voice had gotten so faint I could barely hear it. "I'm sorry."

"Useless sport with a useless team."

"Daddy . . ."

"You are useless, Dagmar! *You're nothing.* Wasting your time with all this. Wasting my time and my good money. And my good carpet. I've never seen anything so useless in my life. Like mother, like daughter. *You're nothing!*"

I looked up to see Paige mouthing the words along with him. *You're nothing!*

"You shut your mouth!" her mother said.

"Don't you get involved," her father said. "You're encouraging her."

"Well, *someone* has to."

"I'm out of here," the un-Dagmar said.

"Don't you walk out on me when I'm talking to you!"

Their voices grew muffled as they moved to another part of the room, away from the wall their apartment shared with Paige's bedroom. More snarling and threatening. More indistinct remarks and asides. I found myself pressing up against the wall, trying to hear. And then wishing I hadn't when I heard what I heard. A cry from the un-Dagmar and then the unmistakable sound of a slap. Skin meeting skin. Paige lowered her eyes, withdrawing into herself as it went on and on and on. It ended with the slamming of a door and a rattling of the wall.

I kept hearing that slam over and over again.

Suddenly, something took hold of me. Snapping the cap back on the marker, I stood up and crossed through the room.

"Janey? Where are you going?"

I didn't answer. I kept walking. Paige scrambled to her feet behind me, following me through the little living room and out into the hallway of the apartment building.

# 21

**Dagmar was there, just like I expected** her to be.

Well. It was the un-Dagmar, really.

She was crumpled against the wall of the hallway, curled up into herself, crying. Her mascara was running down the sides of her face in long black streaks. Her soccer uniform was rumpled up. There was a pink blotch on her cheek, just beginning to swell. And she was cradling something against her belly. It was pinkish-purple and white, with long, furry . . .

Ears?

A rabbit?

It was a stuffed bunny. With a hard, jewel-bright magenta nose and a fuzzy white belly. Its eyes were enormous and blue. Well, its *eye*. Singular. It only had one. From the looks of it, the other had been ripped out, leaving behind a hastily patched rip, some cotton stuffing poking out.

The un-Dagmar wasn't a queen. Not anymore.

On the other side of the wall, her parents were still arguing.

"I won't be treated this way in my own home!" her father said.

"Then get out! Just get out!" her mother shot back. "You like it better at the bar anyway."

"Maybe I will."

"Oh yeah?"

"Maybe I'll go farther than that!"

"Try it!"

"And what'll you do?"

"Take you for every penny you have, that's what!"

"So you can spoil Dagmar."

"So I can watch you suffer!"

Between the two of them going at it and the dim light of the hallway, it was a second or two before Dagmar realized Paige and I were there. When she saw us, I could almost hear the sound of her hardened mask clamping down into place. In a sweep, she was up on her feet, backing away from us, hiding the stuffed animal behind her back.

"What are you doing here?" she said.

It was a good question. I found myself looking back to Paige, still hovering near the doorway of her own apartment. She shook her head. I turned back to Dagmar. Her nose was swollen and red, the dull light making her upper lip glisten with snot.

*Is something wrong, Dagmar?*

The words came back to me from some tiny corner of my memory. The day that Caitlyn first stopped Dagmar from picking on Paige. The words that had seemed so ridiculous to me at the time. How could anything be wrong when you were Dagmar Hagen? That was what I'd asked myself.

Now I knew.

"Is something wrong, Dagmar?" I asked softly.

Dagmar paused, and I could tell she was struggling with the peculiar predicament. Obviously, she wasn't okay. We could all see her crying. And the fact that we'd come out of Paige's apartment clearly meant that we'd heard everything. That we were still hearing everything. But I knew she didn't want to admit to it. It was only that she couldn't think of an easy answer that we wouldn't all know was a lie.

She settled with deflection. "It's none of your business."

"I know," I said. "I just . . ."

"You just *what*?"

I faltered.

"Did you want to come laugh?" She gestured to the door behind her. "Enjoy the show?"

"No."

"Maybe feel better about yourself?"

"No!"

"Leave me alone, *freak*!"

"I just—"

She tilted her face forward, eyes bulging. "Just *what*?"

"I'm sorry." A pause. "And, if you need to talk to some-one or something, I could listen."

I don't think it was the response she'd been expecting. Dagmar pulled back, folding her arms around her middle, the rabbit pressed against her stomach. "I don't want to talk about it."

"Are you lying?" I asked, echoing my dad's words.

Dagmar was silent for a moment. I almost thought she was going to say yes, but then she shook her head. "No," she said.

"Are you sure?" It was Paige who spoke up, taking a hesitant half step out of her doorway.

Dagmar nodded, sniffling. "Just leave me alone."

Paige and I looked at each other. What else could we do? "Okay," I said, feeling like that was the wrong answer.

Using the sleeve of her uniform, she wiped the tears and runny mascara from her eyes. A second swipe smeared the snot from under her nose. "You say anything about this and you're dead. You hear me? You're dead!"

"I'm not going to."

"Good." She nodded once, then her eyes darted to Paige, just over my shoulder. "And *you*," she said. "You better not try anything again."

*Again?*

"I won't," Paige said, for what I was suddenly sure was not the first time. "You know I won't."

"You *and* your nosy family."

Finally, I understood.

I understood Dagmar Hagen. It wasn't that I could forgive her for what she'd done to Paige in the past, but I could see why, at last, she'd pick Paige. Paige, who was sweet and kind and had never done anything to hurt her. It wasn't about what Paige was, it was about what Paige *knew*. When you had a secret, you had to silence the person who knew your secret.

It was a strangely intimate relationship, between the bully and the bullied. I'd never realized it before.

More than that, I saw why Dagmar felt the need to be large and in charge at school. She had to be in control of one small part of her life, because she clearly had no control over the rest of it. It was just like the stories my dad would sometimes tell me about people kicking animals. His office would often see cats and dogs that people had abused, just so they could feel like they weren't quite so powerless.

It was like I was looking into Dagmar's soul.

"Good," she said again. She'd gotten the answer she wanted, but Dagmar still looked ready to explode. Her parents had moved their fight deeper into the apartment, leaving the hallway eerily quiet. She breathed heavily, eyes sweeping back and forth between us for a second, her arms shaking as she hugged her stuffed rabbit. I wondered if she could read my mind, see herself the way I was seeing her for the first time. "Well, what are you still doing out here?"

"Nothing," I said. "I just wanted to know—"

"Get out!"

"What?

"Go *away*."

I felt Paige's hand on my shoulder, pulling me back in the direction of her apartment. "C'mon, Janey."

"But."

"C'mon."

Surrendering, I started to let Paige pull me back inside.

Just as we were about to cross the threshold, though, I pulled away from her, going back over to Dagmar in three easy strides.

And I gave her a hug.

I can't say what I expected, exactly. I'd never imagined ever hugging Dagmar Hagen. But to my surprise, my skin didn't blister, crack, and peel. My sleeves didn't catch on fire. Dagmar was human; made of flesh and bone. Same as me and Paige and Caitlyn. I felt her muscles tense for half a second before she actually relaxed. She didn't hug me back or anything like that. But she didn't hurt me either. She just stood there.

Like she was accepting what I had to give.

After a moment, I pulled away from her. "You're not nothing," I whispered.

The two of us locked eyes. She snuffled again, burying her face in the sleeve of her uniform, but as she did, I could have sworn I heard her mutter, "Thank you."

The door shut behind Paige with a click and she turned the lock before flopping against it, looking shaken. On the other side, muffled by a sleeve and a stuffed rabbit, we could sort of hear Dagmar crying again.

"I didn't know," I said quietly. About her parents. About her dad. About her life. About the very vulnerable and frightened girl who lived in Dagmar Hagen's bruised skin.

Paige shook her head. "No one does. No one except us."

Suddenly I remembered a day in the cafeteria, what felt like ages ago. When I made the choice to sit down with Paige. That song she'd been singing, "The Girl Next Door"...

*The demons are people*
*And the people are demons*
*And the scales of justice*
*Will never be even*

Paige had not only known, but she'd been struggling with what she'd known for a long time, letting it peek out in song, like the stuffing of Dagmar's bunny peeking out from the missing eye. "And that's why she hates you," I said.

"She hates my whole family." Paige sighed. "My mom once called the police about it."

"And they didn't do anything?"

"Dagmar swore up and down the street that all the bruises were from soccer practice."

"And the police believed that?"

"The reporting officer was April's dad. He's seen how hard Dagmar plays on the field."

I started to nod. And then something came crashing down on me. "You brought me here on purpose. Tonight. You wanted me to hear that. You've known all along and you needed me to know."

"Yeah," Paige admitted. "I think so."

"Have you done this before? To other people?"

"No. Never." She struggled, a line forming between her eyes as she tried to figure out what it was she wanted to say. "I never thought anyone else needed to understand Dagmar. The way I do. Not until what happened. What she did to you today."

I felt like a dog in a kennel, trapped in too small a space. I needed to move. I started to pace back and forth across the entryway to Paige's apartment, flexing my fingers at my sides. I could hear Tyrone's cartoons in the next room, drowning out the sounds from the rest of the building. Covering up the yelling and the fighting and the hitting and the crying. "We have to do something."

"What?"

What? I struggled, trying to come up with the answer. "There has to be something." I hadn't realized how used to being a person of action I had become. *"Something."* But this time holding doors open and offering free mints wasn't going to work. Nor was I in a position to put myself between a victim and a bully. Not when the bully was a full-grown man.

What would Caitlyn do?

I had no idea.

"We can't just stand by and let it happen."

But that was what I'd always done. Stood by and let things happen. I'd spent my whole life as the constant bystander.

"There's nothing we can do, Janey," Paige said.

"Then I'll find someone who *can* do something."

She opened her mouth. And for a second, I thought she was going to point out once more that I was obviously powerless. Instead, she nodded. "Okay."

Well. That was . . . easy. I nodded too. "Good."

"With you on my side, it just might work."

"You think?"

"You are so different, Janey," she said. "From before, I mean."

"I guess."

"You know where that comes from?"

Yeah. I did.

Paige nodded again. "Okay. We'll tell someone."

"Okay."

"After the dance," she said. "Let Dagmar have her night as queen."

"Are you sure?"

"Yes."

I wasn't entirely convinced that waiting was a good idea. Who knew what else her father could do to her in just a few days? Not to mention the fact that we could lose our nerve. But I surrendered. It seemed only fair. And since we didn't know where to begin, we could use the time to figure it out. "All right."

Paige sank down to the floor. I moved to sit next to her. For a while, we were silent together. It was all a lot to take in, both what we'd witnessed and what we were planning to do. But somewhere in the back of my head, I heard my dad laughing, reminding me that being a superhero was never easy.

Had I become one overnight? Had I somehow crossed the threshold from sidekick to hero?

Wasn't that something?

I didn't deserve the mantle. Not after the way I'd treated my mentor. I needed to make that up to her.

An idea started to form. Absently, I twisted the marker that I was still holding. I pulled off the cap, drawing an insignia on the back of my hand, an insignia that I'd seen in one of my dad's comic books. Just one little star-shaped symbol made the difference in how a normal person was seen by the world at large. Just one little image took that person across the line from ordinary to extraordinary. It gifted that person with the title of hero. It made that person superlative.

Supreme.

Sensational.

Special.

"Are you going to the dance?" I asked Paige.

"No," she said, shaking her head. "No one asked me."

"Me neither."

"Really?" She sounded genuinely surprised. "I heard that Tyler was going to ask you."

I shrugged, barely registering it. "Well, he didn't. How about we go together?"

Paige eyed me critically. "You know everyone will just make fun of us."

"Yeah," I said. "But who cares?"

She smirked a little. "Okay."

"But I need your help with something."

"What?"

"I have an idea, something I want to do," I said, examining the drawing on my hand. "But it's going to take a lot of help. We'd have to talk to Tyler and April and Raquel and all the others from today."

"Janey. What are you thinking?"

"I want to do something. For someone that I've wronged."

"Captain Superlative?"

I wasn't all that surprised that Paige knew we were on bad terms. "Yeah."

Paige nodded. "Good. You two need to patch things up."

"I know."

"Especially since you're running out of time."

That one threw me. "What?"

"Well, I mean . . . since she's . . ."

"She's what?"

"Sick."

*Sick.*

The weight hanging in the middle. Like the vowel sound was stuck on a piece of gum, gluing the word in the air.

I stared at Paige for a full minute. "How did you know?"

"Janey . . ." Her voice was gentle. "You can see it."

"You can?"

She shrugged. "I know I can. And some others are starting to see it too. She's been sitting out of gym for weeks. And . . ."

"And what?"

"And her wig fell off during Science. A couple of us saw. Tyler saw."

I felt red heat rising in my cheeks. It was hard to accept the possibility that I'd been so blind to what was right in front of me. But then, this wasn't exactly the first time. I hadn't really seen Dagmar before. Or Paige. Or, maybe most tragically, myself. Not until very recently. "Oh."

Paige seemed to be reading my mind. She gave me a sympathetic grimace and touched my arm. "What's the plan?"

"Plan?"

"For the dance."

"The dance. Right."

And I told her. I told her exactly what I was thinking. I

told her, and I knew from her smile and her knowing eyes that it was a good idea. Maybe my first one ever. Possibly my last. But if it was my last, I was certainly going to go out with a bang. And I wasn't going to be alone.

# 22

**Someone very wise had once said to** me that I got my heroic streak from my dad, because he was a super-duper, first-rate sort of guy. But I wasn't the only one who'd picked up a few super-duper qualities from a parent. When Mrs. Li saw me at the door, I wouldn't have blamed her at all if she'd slammed it shut in my face. I would have deserved it. And worse. I can't imagine what she must have thought of me showing up unannounced one day, storming out without saying good-bye, leaving her daughter in tears, then reappearing two days later on a Friday afternoon. I know I would have been disgusted with me. But she apparently shared her daughter's forgiving nature.

"Hello, Jane," she said as she opened the door.

"Hello," I said, ducking my head meekly.

"Come inside, come inside."

"Thanks." She stepped out of the way and I followed her into the entry hall, slipping out of my shoes without being told this time. I put them by the red high-top sneakers. And by my other pair of shoes, the ones I'd abandoned two days before.

I tried not to look at them. Mrs. Li pointedly didn't say anything about it.

"Can I get you some tea?"

"No, thank you."

"Are you sure?"

"I'd like to talk to Caitlyn. It's kind of important."

Mrs. Li nodded. "You can go upstairs."

"Thanks."

She opened her mouth, as if to say something more. I don't know. Maybe to politely ask me not to make her daughter cry again. But whatever it was, she didn't say it.

"Don't worry," I told her.

She seemed to accept that.

The curtains were open in Caitlyn's room. The misty February light flooding in through the windows gave it a dreamy brightness. She was sitting by the windows in her pink pj's with a purple polka-dot scarf wrapped around her head, resting her chin on the sill as she looked out. I knew in an instant that she'd seen me come running up the driveway. And I didn't need to announce myself at the threshold of her door. She could feel me behind her shoulder.

"Are you going to yell at me again, Janey?" she asked dully, without looking back at me.

"No," I said.

"Good."

She continued to stare out the window. The silence was uncomfortable. But I didn't say a word. I waited, letting her think. Her sleeves were rolled up. I noticed a pale, pinkish rash on her left arm in the bend of her elbow. She scratched at it absently. I knew now that it was a symptom of her disease. I'd hesitantly approached my dad, as mild as Selina, and asked him to tell me about leukemia. I thought it might upset him, scratch up the ghost of my mother, but he'd been incredibly patient and understanding about the whole thing. My admiration for Caitlyn Li had swollen like a balloon. It seemed like nothing but spit and paper clips were holding her together.

And her incredible force of will.

"I'm not completely delusional, you know," she finally said, turning to look over at me. She seemed so impossibly tired. "I know I'm not a real superhero."

I took that as my invitation and stepped into the room, setting my bag down by the door. I opened it, pulling out the latest issue of *Hawkgirl*. I'd picked it up on my way over. "I don't know," I said, perching myself on the foot of her bed, looking down at the glossy cover.

"What?"

"Maybe you are. From everything my dad's told me about superheroes, you fit the profile. I mean, you do have a tragic origin story."

She smiled faintly. "I do."

"And a secret identity." I paused. And then shook my head. "Well, not so secret, I guess."

That made her laugh. Just a little. "Uh-huh."

"And a sidekick."

The laughter faded. She pulled her legs up onto the window seat, hugging her knees to her chest. She was so small. Folded up like that, she looked like I could pick her up and put her in my pocket. And keep her. "Not lately," she said. "I had one for a while, but she got it into her head that I was some kind of selfish coward. Or something like that."

Or something like that. Looking back on my anger, even I couldn't exactly explain it. Probably because it had come from a place of fear instead of real anger. Fear for my own existence as a seventh-grade pariah. Fear of losing the best friend I'd ever had. "I'm sorry," I said.

The words weren't nearly enough of an apology. "Thanks," she said anyway. That was what superheroes were supposed to do. Defend and protect the imperfect, like me.

"I shouldn't have said all those things," I raced on, thirsty for her forgiveness. "I don't know what I was thinking."

"Stop." She held up a hand.

"I'm sorry."

"I know."

Of course she did. I smiled slightly, staring down at my hand. The superhero symbol I'd drawn yesterday had faded, but I could still see its outline. "I think that I understand things better now."

"Now that you know the truth about me?"

"Yeah."

"That I'm sick."

I didn't want that to be the truth about her. And it wasn't. It was only a small part of it. "You're sick. And no one can help you. And... and there's no feeling worse than when no one can help you." She'd flat-out told me that. I just hadn't been listening. "That's why you do it. That's why you're a superhero. That's why you were helping Paige and everyone else. So they don't have to feel like you do."

She stood up from her seat, walking over to sit next to me on the bed. Her weight felt unbearably heavy beside me. Spit and paper clips holding her together. And her incredible force of will. "I knew you were special, Janey," she said, reaching out to touch my arm with her thin, bony fingers. "That's why you had to be the one. Superlative."

"Life is too short to be anything less."

"Exactly."

"There is one thing I don't understand, though."

"What?"

"If you're so sick, why on earth are you still going to school? I mean, I'd be so out of there."

She laughed. "Because," she said, "I decided that I wanted to be a superhero. You can't do that sitting all alone in bed."

"True."

"And the principal said I could. As long as I didn't disrupt classes or anything."

"Really?"

"Yeah."

That made me smile. So the teachers *were* in on it. That felt kind of nice now. Like they'd given us the gift of Captain Superlative. "Cool."

"My parents think I'm crazy," she added, grimacing.

"But they're letting you do it anyway?"

"Well, I still get my mom's trademark 'neutral disappointed face' every time I come down to dinner in my cape. But they came around. Eventually."

Somehow that didn't surprise me. She could probably convince a rainy day to let in the sun. "I'd like things to go back," I said.

"Back?"

"To the way they were. I don't think I've ever been as happy as I was when I was being your sidekick."

"Really?"

"Yeah."

She grinned. "It was a lot of fun, wasn't it?"

"Yeah."

"And we were a good team."

"The best." I really meant that.

She gave my arm a gentle squeeze before letting go. "I wish we could go back. We can't."

I felt my stomach drop a little bit. "Can't?"

"No."

"Why not?"

She tilted her head to look at me sideways. "I think you know why not."

She was right. And I hated it. But my dad had explained quite a lot about leukemia. Including the unfair odds, especially for JMML. Odds that even an incredible force of will might not be able to beat. But the world was always spinning forward. There were doctors and scientists and new discoveries every day. I wanted to hope. I needed to hope. "Isn't there anything..."

"Someone can do?" she finished for me.

"Yeah."

She leaned back on her palms. "Well. Yes. There is something. Something that *you* can do."

I blinked in surprise. "Me?"

"You."

"What?" I wasn't a doctor. I was just a vet's kid. A vet's kid who, up until very recently, had been nothing more than air.

"All the stuff we've done in the school," she said. "I don't want it to go away. When I do. I need you to try, Janey."

"Try?"

"Be superlative."

Oh.

*Oh.*

At once, I understood what it was she was asking me. But she didn't even have to ask. "It won't go away," I said, without a trace of uncertainty or hesitation. "Believe me, it won't. I promise."

Things had *changed*.

It's entirely possible she was a little bit surprised by my quick reply. "Good. Good. That's good." She paused. "That's why all superheroes have sidekicks, you know."

"Why?"

She nodded to the nightstand, where her wig lay in a crumpled mess. "Someone has to take up the mantle."

I laughed, a little happily, a little sadly. My idea from the night before was growing and growing, but I didn't want to tell her about it. Not yet. It would be a surprise. The surprise of a lifetime, I was sure. "I don't think I could ever fill your shoes," I said.

"Well," she said, "not if you keep wearing those ugly Blue Shoes."

This time the laughter was all out of joy. "Oh, those things are history, believe me."

"Good. Anyway, don't try to fill my shoes. Find your own shoes. Just maybe ones that lead you to doing good sometimes, okay?"

"Okay," I said, wiggling my toes a little to make her laugh.

We talked for hours after that. Not about superheroes or leukemia or Blue Shoes. We shed all of those external trappings, everything on the outside that didn't really matter, and were just ourselves.

I talked about my mother. I'd never really talked about her before with anyone. We didn't talk about her death, of course. Because neither of us wanted her to be defined in that way. But I shared my memories about her. The headboard. The necklace. The way that she used to make my dad smile, which I saw shadows of from time to time when he was pleased with something that I'd done.

"I have this one memory," I said. "It's not exactly a memory. I can only see her eyes. Brown. Like mine. Looking at me. Down. From the stars. Like we were lying on the front lawn, staring up at the sky or something." But I wasn't sure it had actually happened. It might have just been something I wanted to be real. "I don't know if it's a memory or a dream."

"It could be both," she said.

"Both. Maybe."

She told me all the things I never knew about her, about her family and her life. About Captain Superlative's real origin story. "My birth name is actually Li Hailan," she said.

"Li Hailan," I repeated, trying to get the pronunciation right.

"*Li* is the most common family name in the world."

If that was true, that was the only thing about her that was common. "Does it mean anything?"

"Li means *plum*. Hailan means *ocean waves* or *ripples*." She made little ripples with her fingertips. "I always felt like one of my parents accidentally dropped a plum into a pond one day and decided on my name."

I laughed. "It's pretty."

"We changed it to Caitlyn when we moved here because it sounded a little like Hailan."

"Why'd you change it at all?"

"To fit in. To be American." She'd always been an outsider, even before she started running around in a cape. A stranger in a strange world. "I was a lot like you," she said. "I didn't want anyone to notice me. I was afraid they would think I was weird, or something."

"What changed?"

"I changed."

It was long past dark when she finally confessed, "I'm kind of tired. I should get some sleep now."

I nodded. "Okay."

"Thanks, Janey."

There was a lot encompassed in that *thanks*. I was pretty sure I understood it all.

"Sure." I stood up, stretching my arms up over my head. I walked over to the nightstand, setting the comic book I'd brought her beneath the little fan. "Hey," I said suddenly, "are you going to go to the dance tomorrow?"

"The Valentine's Day dance?" she said, scooting back on her hands until she hit her pile of pillows. "I wouldn't miss it for the world."

"Good," I said, pulling the strap of my bag across my shoulder. "Then I'll see you there."

And maybe surprise her a little.

Or a lot.

Nothing less than a superlative would do.

# 23

**It had snowed the night before. The** walkway leading up to the front doors of Deerwood Park Middle School was coated in a silver sheen. Large and lazy snowflakes continued to fall sporadically, like little pieces of dryer lint, from the trees and streetlights. The janitor had sloshed blue antifreeze into the snowbanks, piled up along the sides of the driveway. It created patterns of melt, the muddy grass and pavement peeking out from the pristine snow—a combination of pretty and ugly, like you find in any middle school.

I could feel my dad watching me in the car's rearview mirror. I looked up, catching his twinkly blue eyes. We had just pulled up into the circle drive out front. The seventh-grade dance was still three hours away, so the school was quiet. No sign of the flood of station wagons and hybrids that would soon descend.

"Are you ready, Janey?" Dad asked, turning over his shoulder to face me. The corners of his eyes were turned up and crinkled.

"Yeah," I said, zipping my coat all the way to my chin.

He reached his arm back between the seats, brushing my hair away from my face. "Try and have a little fun tonight."

"That's the idea."

"I'm proud of you, Janey."

"I know."

He winked.

I let myself out of the car, lugging two bulky and misshapen garbage bags with me. I watched him drive away before I made my way through the front doors. I was wearing thick purple boots, and while all the other girls would probably stop in the entry hall to kick off their boots and slide on ridiculously high heels, I kept right on walking, leaving wet footprints behind me as I made my way into the cafeteria.

It was decorated all in pale pink: pink paper snowflakes, pink fairy lights, pink tablecloths, pink heart-shaped confetti, little pink cupids on streamers. Even billowing pink sheets draped over the doorways, like awnings. The regular tables had been cleared away, replaced with smaller, round tables with pink plastic chairs. "Isn't it pretty?" Paige asked, sidling up beside me. She was wearing pink too—an elegant rose-colored lace dress. Her hair was piled up on top of her head in an elaborate series of braids, which revealed a heart-shaped cutout in the back of her dress. Pink slippers that she'd borrowed from her sister. Pink stud earrings. She even had light pink lipstick. We'd gotten ready together at her place, a few hours before. I'd needed her help putting together an outfit for myself and putting the final touches on my plan.

Our plan.

"Yeah," I said, giving her a hug like we hadn't seen each other in weeks. "It's pretty."

"But?"

I gave her a mischievous grin out of the side of my mouth. "But I think it could use more in the way of color."

"Yeah," Paige said slowly, a smile stretching out across her face. "Yeah, I think you're right."

"Want to do something about it?"

Paige nodded before taking my hand and leading me over to the door of the cafeteria. Sitting in a neat pile, just outside in the hallway, were three bulky bags like mine. "I told Tyler and the others to get here early so we could coordinate everything and practice," she said. "They should show up any minute."

"Great," I said, setting down my bags and opening them. "Then let's get ready for them."

It was rare for any kind of event at Deerwood Park Middle School to begin on time, but much to the teachers' surprise, almost everyone was in the cafeteria by the official start of the dance, so the music was already playing. I could hear kids chatting and laughing as I bundled up the empty garbage bags and shoved them into my locker. The only kids I hadn't seen yet were Dagmar, who liked to arrive fashionably late, and Captain Superlative, who I knew had a doctor's appointment to go to first.

With a deep breath, I looked at my reflection in the little mirror inside of my locker. *Janey*, I said quietly to myself, *you can do this*.

The girl looking back at me wasn't even a little bit afraid.

She was smiling.

Paige was waiting for me when I came back to the cafeteria doors. And when I took off my coat, she held out her hands to take it from me.

I walked on alone.

Even though a lot of kids knew about my plan, I hadn't told *everyone*. And we definitely hadn't warned any of the teacher chaperones. So it was only natural that some of the voices around me fell silent in surprise as I walked through the room. I felt eyes on me.

What difference did it make?

I came to a stop in the center of the cafeteria, so absolutely everyone could see me. I was wearing a bright blue bathing suit over purple tights, disappearing into my purple boots. I'd borrowed my dad's blue dish gloves, along with a thick brown belt with an enormous gold buckle. And flowing down my back from my shoulders was a cape made of a blue pillowcase with a purple felt *J* glued into the center. I'd decorated it with artistic swooshes and swirls. And dozens upon dozens of little stars.

No mask.

Tyler was the first to join me. He hurried over, giving

me that smile of his that made girls melt. He was wearing a nice button-down shirt and a pair of jeans. Draped over his shoulders was a cape that I'd made out of Selina's blanket. Kevin hobbled out with him on his crutches, wearing a matching outfit. The only difference was that his cape was one that Paige had put together from one of her mother's kerchiefs. And Kevin had taped paper lightning bolts to the crutches too.

Paige followed after them, throwing a green cape over her shoulders. It was really a canvas grocery bag, but together we'd added a big letter *P* to it, drawn out of flowering vines and leaves. You would have thought that the green of the cape and the pink of her dress would have clashed, but they didn't. Paige looked like a flower.

One by one, other kids joined. They wore their dresses and ties and high-heeled shoes. Their blazers and flowy skirts and loafers. But they wore capes too. Capes that Paige and I had brought. Capes that Tyler and Raquel and April and the others had scavenged from old dress-up clothes and bathroom towels and printer paper. Some of them had gloves. Some wore domino masks. I even spotted one girl wearing a bicycle helmet decorated with superhero stickers.

Once upon a time, before Captain Superlative, we'd all been the same. Now, when we couldn't have looked more different, for the first time ever, we were *unified*.

We were all superheroes. Every last one of us.

Well... almost all of us.

There was a loud, strangled gasp and we turned to see

Dagmar standing in the doorway, wearing a stunning red dress and a look of shock. "You have got to be kidding me," she said.

Well, it was now or never.

I grabbed a nearby chair and pulled it out from the table, brushing some confetti off the seat before I stood up on top of it, my boots squeaking loudly. I raised my hands, making myself bigger. A teacher chaperone tensed, obviously uncomfortable with my precarious position. "My name," I said, fighting the dryness in my throat, "is Super J! And I'm here to save the day!"

Tyler was next. He cleared his throat and everyone turned to look at him, giving him the chance to strike a dramatic pose. He held it for a second before he pulled a comb out of his pocket and ran it through his hair. "My name is T-Bird," he said. "And I'm here to spread the word!" He struck another pose, pointing his comb out at the crowd.

He really *was* a ham.

There were a few giggles from the girls on the sidelines. Then April jumped up, twirling to show off her pink cape, one she'd pulled from our old stash of dress-up clothes. "My name is Amazo Girl!" she said. "And I'm going to use my powers . . . to change the world!"

"April!" Dagmar ran into the cafeteria, like she wanted to plow her down. There was a pained look of betrayal on her face.

The room exploded. Suddenly everyone was throwing in their own catchphrase, too eager and excited to wait their turns. Some of them were really clever. "My name is

Power Guy, and I'll help anyone who meets my eye!" Others were just downright silly. "They call me Coolio Cool. I'm the coolest cool kid in the school!" But each was unique. Each belonged to the person who created it. No two kids were the same.

In the excitement, I saw Dagmar trembling with emotion. Rage, maybe. For the first time, she was the outsider, she was the one who didn't quite follow the trend. I thought she might start to cry. Standing there, in her formal dress, she was a perfect reflection of the girl I'd seen in the hallway of the apartment building.

Alone.

But to my surprise, Paige walked over to her, carrying a bundled-up kitchen apron in her hands. It was the last of our capes, and I realized all at once that Paige had set it aside, had been holding on to it. Saving it for Dagmar. And as Dagmar turned to look at her, Paige offered it up.

I didn't see if she took it, though.

"Will you be superlative?" I shouted, cupping my hands around my mouth.

"Yes, we will!" my friends replied, just like we'd practiced.

"Will you be superlative?" I said again.

"Yes, we will!" my friends said again, this time joined by others.

"Will you be superlative?"

"Yes, we will!"

I couldn't be sure, but I thought that everyone said it that last time. It was followed up by an enormous cheer. All at once the kids who hadn't been part of the scheme were improvising capes. They grabbed the tablecloths, scattering confetti. A couple boys tried to pull down one of the pink awnings, until the teachers grabbed them by the shoulders, pulling them away. I was probably facing a million years of detention for what I'd started.

It was worth it.

It was worth it to see my classmates—my *friends*—like this. Falling over themselves to be superlative.

With a crack, the door to the cafeteria swung open. "Citizens!" Captain Superlative's voice boomed through the room as she bounded inside, back in her cape and mask and wig. To look at her, you'd never have thought she was sick. She was overflowing with energy and excitement. "I've returned to—"

And then she saw us.

And then she saw *me*.

We turned to stare at each other, holding a look. For a second, I was uncertain. She was frozen on some kind of event horizon, all expression lost under her mask. But the spell broke and she let out a triumphant laugh, running, sprinting, leaping across the floor between us, cape fluttering in the air. The crowd parted and cheered. I jumped down from the chair just in time to let her throw her arms around me.

"You did all this!" It wasn't a question.

"*We* did," I said.

She pulled back to look at me, her hands clasped around my elbows.

"Superhero is the new normal."

She pulled me in tight for another hug. I don't know how

everyone reacted to that. I was too busy hugging her back. And then we were too busy laughing. I was only just dimly aware of a chant rising up behind me:

"Janey! Janey! Janey!"

# Epilogue

**The paper lanterns winked out one by** one. Only the fiercest ones kept rising, trying to jockey for a position among the stars. And slowly, kids began to file away from the parking lot, shepherded back into the SUVs by parents or older siblings. Tomorrow was the Fourth of July. There would be a parade and a carnival and barbecues and touch-football games. So much to do. So much running and laughing and playing.

So much life.

Somewhere behind me, I heard my dad talking to Officer Cormack and his "best friend" April. He was really on a roll, and I knew we wouldn't be leaving for some time. Which, quite frankly, was fine with me. I kept my eyes on the sky, walking over to a stretch of grass that ran alongside the parking lot. Paige followed after me.

A little shrine had been set up, with flameless candles and photographs of Captain Superlative. There were flowers and a few stuffed animals and lots of cards for the Li family. A bunch of comic books. And capes made of a thousand different things. I added my plastic tiara from the Valentine's Day dance to the collection, remembering how, as Valentine's Day queen, I could have asked anyone I wanted to dance the last dance with me. I could have had Tyler, but I'd chosen Captain Superlative instead.

I gave her my drawing too. The first one I'd ever done of her, on the shopping-list notepad: Captain Superlative, shooting through the sky, surrounded by stars and comets and spinning planets with dozens of twirling moons. Maybe it wasn't my best drawing—I'd done hundreds more since joining the art club—but it was still my favorite.

I also left a valentine, the one I'd crumpled up in my room. I'd found it a week ago, lost in a corner.

Paige offered up a handful of mints.

There were ten times as many tributes online. A new hashtag—#WillYouBeSuperlative—had gotten pretty popular. I was gratified about that, really. The memorial we'd set up by the school would eventually fade away. Flowers would wilt. Electric candles would run out of juice. The rest would be cleared away, sent off to the Li family. But what we'd started online would last.

Or that was the theory, anyway.

Paige and I lay down on our backs, side by side on the lawn. The blades of grass bristled against my arms and legs.

"How did you find out?" I asked her. No need to explain what I meant.

*She's gone.*

"Phone tree," she said. "Tyler's mom called Kevin's mom, who called my mom. Don't know who she told."

I nodded slightly, grateful that Paige didn't ask me how I found out. It had been a call directly from Mrs. Li.

But I knew before that. I just woke up that morning and felt like the world had dried up a little bit. It was a comfort, because when the call came, it wasn't a surprise. Just a confirmation of what I already knew. It was my permission to cry, to curl up in my dad's arms and be his baby again. For a little while.

"She came over and told *my* mom."

Paige and I turned our heads to see Dagmar. She was wearing shorts and a tank top. She could now, because she no longer had bruises to hide. After Paige and I told my dad the truth, something happened. I didn't know what, and I was okay with that. It was bigger than me. What mattered was that I'd said something at all. The days of people seeing something and not doing anything about it were over in Deerwood Park. At least now that we were eighth graders and in charge of the school.

At least, I hoped.

Dagmar stretched out on the grass beside Paige, looking up at the sky with us. The wounds she'd inflicted on Paige—the invisible ones born out of torment and insults—would never heal completely. I could see that in the way Paige's body tensed and then untensed. But they were scabbing over. Which was something. And I could tell that Dagmar noticed too. "It's too hot," she said irritably, in her brattiest voice.

"Yeah," Paige said. She allowed herself to turn back to the sky.

We lay there in silence, watching as the little flames in the night sky vanished from sight, the lanterns going wherever it was they went in the end. "Do you think I should have said something?" I asked them.

Paige looked over at me. "Like what?"

I shrugged. "I don't know. A speech of some kind." I was the right one to do it, I knew. I was her sidekick, and I would be the one to take up her mantle. "Like that she wouldn't have wanted us to be sad or something like that."

"We're sad," Dagmar said. "That's just the way it is."

"I guess." I scowled a little. "What would she do?"

"Offer free hugs," Dagmar replied, toeing off her Blue Shoes to run the soles of her feet along the grass.

"And mints," Paige said. "Calling this a test of our courage, or something."

I smiled up at the sky. "Yeah."

Another moment of silence washed over us. "I wrote a song," Paige said in a small voice. "I felt like I ought to sing for her."

"Why didn't you?" Dagmar asked.

"I don't know," Paige said. "I guess I was just waiting for when the time felt right."

Dagmar shrugged a little bit. "What's wrong with now?"

Paige nodded slightly. I heard her start humming, searching for her song out of nothingness. Dagmar and I both turned to watch her. Neither of us could do what Paige did. I think we were in awe of her superpower:

*When life crashes on your shore*
*When it grinds you through a sieve*
*Turn your face into the storm*
*And inside you I'll live*

*Never let anyone define you*
*Have the courage to forgive*
*Hold every door wide open*
*And inside you I'll live*

*This echo is my legacy*
*And it's all I have to give*
*So remember all the things I've taught you*
*And inside you I'll live*

*And inside you I'll be*
*Superlative*

We lapsed into silence. It wasn't the silence that came from absence. We were thinking, remembering. And as we lay there, the sky crackled once. A fine, misty rain started to fall, silvering the grass and the three of us. All four elements came together, the rainwater on us as we lay on the earth, watching the fire in the sky. Soon, only one light remained.

Or maybe it was a star.

# Acknowledgments

**I have to start by thanking my mother.** You'll see why in a moment.

There are so many superlative people who contributed to the work of *Captain Superlative* taking flight. I thank my extraordinary agent, Brianne Johnson at Writers House, for starting the journey and my wonderful Disney Hyperion editor, Tracey Keevan, for guiding the way.

No writer will get anywhere without some amazing teachers, so I thank Betty Grossman, Jennifer Franklin Ferrari, and Rives Collins for putting me on this path. Every sentence I write is touched by what you taught me. Without Esther Hershenhorn, I might never have cracked the mystery that is Janey. And thank you to Jennie Y. Jiang and Xiaomeng Zhou for helping me polish and fine-tune Captain Superlative's secret identity.

Thank you to the exceptional individuals who helped to refine Captain Superlative's story, both as a play and then as a novel: Douglas Post and everyone in his class at Chicago Dramatists; Savannah Couch and the cast and crew at the Purple Crayon Players' PLAYground Festival of Fresh Works; Stephen Fredericks and the folks at the Growing Stage Theatre; Madelyn Sergel, Madeline Franklin, and the cast and crew at the Clockwise Theatre; and most especially, the members of my UChicago Graham School Writer's Studio writing group, Klariza Alvaran, Lisa Sukenic, Jennifer Tobias, Alena Weicher, Jean Williams, and the fearless and fabulous Carly Ho.

I could not have told the story of someone so unapologetically herself without so many such people in my life. A big thanks to Jen Cowhy, Faye Kroshinsky, David Johnson, and all my colleagues at the University of Chicago Consortium on School Research, who care about helping children more than anyone I've ever known and whose research guided me on all points of school safety and adolescent trauma. Thank you to my fellow writers Jessica Cluess, Meg Bullock, and Mia McCullough for believing in me when I didn't believe in myself; to Stephanie Kaplan, Kara Downey, Robby Forbes-Karol, Nancy Waites, and Karen Fraley for never doubting me, even when I was being a neurotic mess of self-doubt. Thank you to my insane friends Nicole Keating, Joshua D. Allard, John and Ronen Kohn, and everyone else at both the Piccolo Theatre and DCP for inspiring me with your outlandish and amazing personalities. And thank you to my entire family, especially Mrs. Gloria Puller.

Finally, thank you to the people who most directly made me me. I thank my father, Neil Puller, who showed me what it means to work hard and to reach for goals. And I thank my mother, Deborah Goldberg, who taught me to be a force for good in the world—and who I promised to thank both first and last when I won my Tony Award. This may not be a Tony, Mom, but it's the greatest prize I could ever ask for.